I0591102

Chance Encounter

TAMZIN ATKINS

Chance Encounter

Flamelightpublishing

Published by Flamelight Publishing
Edited by Tamzin Atkins
Cover Art by Mellissa Hofmann

ISBN: 978-0-7961-7451-2(print)

978-0-7961-7452-9(e-book)

Dedication

I dedicate this book to my boyfriend, Shervaan Baros, for always supporting me,and encouraging me to be a better writer. To my best friend, and person, Amy Esterhuizen, for always being there for me. To Lariska Kruis for always listening to me, and giving me advice. Finally, to my family for always allowing me to follow my dreams, and a shout out to all those loyal supporters who read my books.

PROLOGUE

Code blue, I repeat, Code blue," shouted a nurse.

In seconds, there was a flurry of movement around the thirty-five-year-old male, lying in a hospital bed, dying. His body shook with spasms, as his heart rate beat out of control. Nurses held him down, to no avail, the heart machine showing no heart beat, the only sound in the room a long, straight beep. A defibrillator was rubbed with cold gel and placed on his chest with low voltage, the body jolting each time to no avail.

"Doctor! What do we do? He is flat-lining," asked the intern.

Gabriel Bennett looked down at the blood soaking his hands; running onto the spotless white floor, turning red. A young woman burst through the doors; screaming and crying.

"Help him, don't let my husband die!" screamed the woman; as two male nurses held her back.

Gabriel looked at the man lying there with the tubes still in his mouth and closed his eyes.

"Why aren't you doing anything?" shouted the woman.

"Call it," said Gabriel, turning to look at the clock.

"But, Sir?"

"I said call it now!"

"Time of death, 3:45 pm," replied the nurse.

"No, you just let him die, you killed him," screamed the woman, collapsing to the floor.

Gabriel walked past the bed, making his way to the door. The woman grabbed onto his bloody shirt. "You just let him die. You killed him. His blood is on your hands" Without another word, he walked out of the room, and out of Newport Memorial Hospital, listening to the screams of a grieving spouse.

Gabriel was startled awake, disoriented and lost for the first few seconds it took for him to adjust. His body trembled with after shock; the dream had been so real that he felt as though he was there again. He took a deep, shuddering breath in and out, as he looked around the place he called home. His hands shook slightly, the memory too close to the surface at the moment. He looked down at his hands; there was no trace of blood on them, and there wouldn't be. He watched the people he called friends, wake up to a new day on the streets. Gabe ran a hand through his longer-than-usual shoulder-length black hair. The drum stood a few feet away from him, the last of last night's smoke evaporating in the air. He turned away from the drum and drew his denim-clad legs up, with his arms resting on his bent knees and his hands hanging between them. This moment right here made it all worth it. He opened his eyes in time to see the sun slowly peeking through the support beams from the bridge above. He loved to watch the way the darkness suddenly became light in an array of colours. The cardboard under him moved slightly with every movement he made. He stared down at his only pair of clothing, torn and dirty with a look of disdain. He had been living here for three years now. It seemed like a life time ago that he had been known as Dr. Bennett. Some things never went away, no matter how hard you had fallen. Every time he looked down at his hands, he saw death, pain, and suffering.

He had pledged to save lives; instead, he had taken one. Most days he wanted to curl up and die, but living like this was his punishment for what he had done. No matter what he did, she still wouldn't have her husband, and her kids still wouldn't have their father. He had robbed them, taken from them something they could never get back, and in return, he had given up his own life to live under a dirty bridge. He listened to the sound of trolley wheels rolling across the cold cement; it was like a soothing balm to his restless soul. Today was an early start for most. It was dustbin day, and that meant it was digging time. If anyone had told him three years ago that he would be digging through his old friend's trash for something to eat, he would have called them crazy and laughed. Now he, like many others, counted the days until dustbin day, praying for people to waste their good food. His own rusted trolley stood next to him, along with all his worldly possessions. To others, it was junk, but to him, it was a way to make money to survive.

Life wasn't about making money, but when you lived on the street, every cent counted. In his trolley was a small battery-operated radio and a couple of glass bottles that he sold for money. There was a cardboard box filled with all his personal photo albums and a few objects from the scrap yard he was hoping to fix up and sell. He stood up with a groan, his bones clicking back in place. He was definitely getting too old to be sleeping on the old floor. He felt older than his thirty-five years of age. A squad car flashed its lights; the driver hooting as it slowly drove by. "Come on, guys, I know it sucks, but it is time to clear out for the day," called the police officer in the car. He stopped the car in one spot, talking to some of the regulars. Gabe admired the man that at least treated them like humans. Gabe slipped on his floor-length, tattered brown jacket that had cost him a fortune new and rolled up his old checkered blanket and placed it into his trolley. He opened and closed his fingers a few times, before blowing out a breath and wrapped his hands around the handle bar. He took one step forward. Today was like most days; his motto the same. Try to survive, even if he didn't feel like he was worth it.

CHAPTER 1

T wenty-seven-year-old Ashley James, stood on the sidewalk outside her apartment building, donned in black jogging shorts and a tank top She turned the music up on her iPod, her headphones blocking out all other sounds. She bent over and touched her toes, counting to ten until her calves started burning slightly from the pressure. She then stood up and stretched her hands above her head, before taking off on her jog down the street. Ashley loved this time of morning, when everyone else was just waking up to start their day, and she was alone with just the street lamps and the rising sun. She smiled to herself and picked up her pace, breathing deeply through her mouth. Ashley stopped and guzzled down half her water bottle in one go, pouring some over her wet blonde hair and down her back. Her black vest top stuck to her skin with sweat and water, cooling rapidly in the morning weather. She stopped at the top of the hill, overlooking the city, and bent down, placing her hands on her knees, as she took in a deep breath. Her stop watch started beeping loudly, she turned to her wrist and looked at the time. She had made it just in time; a minute or two later and she would have missed it. She stood up and looked straight ahead.

The sun rose in the distance, between two high-rise buildings, as they reflected off the sides in an array of vast colours. Ashley stood there alone on the sidewalk watching all this happen. She watched the sunrise most mornings when she was not on shift or had a late morning like today, and yet it still left her in awe of the beauty of it all. Every day, no matter what happened, or what went wrong, the sun still rose between those two buildings. She turned around and made her way back home at a much slower pace, taking her time to watch the neighbourhood come to life.

Ashley made her way into her one-bedroom apartment, locking the door behind her and stripping off her sweaty clothes as she went. They hit the wooden floors with a loud smacking sound, lying in a small puddle. She walked naked into the bathroom and switched on the shower, humming a tune, as she waited for the water to heat up. The room filled with thick steam around her. Ashley let her hair down and stepped into the glass shower. She moaned in pleasure, as the water soothed her muscles. Ashley checked the time and slipped on her uniform before grabbing a juicy red apple from the fruit bowl. She locked the door and started down the stairs. Half way down; her cell phone rang in her pocket. She pulled it out and groaned with loud emphasis in the empty hallway, before answering her older brother's call. Ashley loved her brother; but hated him meddling in her life. "Before you say anything, big brother, I am about to go into work and start a shift," said Ashley, with a roll of her eyes at his grumblings.

"Ash, it's Dad!" started her brother Chad.

Ashley suddenly stopped mid-step, her heart beating frantically as she grabbed onto the railing for support. That one word said it all, the one person she wished to never speak of again. The silence between them grew awkward and uncomfortable by the second. She sat down on the steps, swallowing repeatedly as she thought of what to say.

"I want you to come home, Ash, please just come home," pleaded Chad.

She squeezed her eyes tightly closed, hearing her older brother beg her for something she couldn't give.

"Did he mention me at all? Did he ask me to come home?" asked Ashley in a whispered tone.

The silence said it all; she took a deep breath and opened her eyes. "Ash, it's not about that, he is very sick at the moment, and you would know more about that than me. Don't you want to be home to say good bye when the time comes?" asked Chad in that soothing tone of his that annoyed her so much, as if he was speaking to a startled child.

"He said that he was ashamed of me, Chad, that he could never look at me again without being disgusted by my lies," mumbled Ashley; her hand flying to cover her mouth as a loud sob escaped.

"He was angry and being stubborn."

"You don't know everything, and besides, he doesn't want me there, Chad, please don't ask this of me," begged Ashley.

"So you don't want to say goodbye?" questioned Chad, his voice rising with his heart-felt pleas.

"I already did," answered Ashley, ending the call before she heard her brother's reply. A loud sob escaped, echoing around her in the empty hallway, tears ran down her cheeks and landing on her knees. Sitting on the dirty step, she sobbed for the father that was close to dying, but dead to her already.

"Ash, did you use two doses of morphine on that older lady yesterday?" asked Romeo.

"No, I used one. I thought you had used it, because it was gone already when I got her settled.," answered Ashley.

He sat down on the bed and looked at her with a stern expression.

"This isn't the first time, Ash, soon, others are going to notice, and then we will have questions to answer, that we don't have answers to. And what is with all these metal flowers? I doubt we are meant to decorate the ambulance, Ash," said Romeo, holding up a beautiful handcrafted flower, made from metal wiring and tin cans.

"Those aren't mine. I think it is our thief saying thank you. But maybe if you stopped flirting with anything on two legs, then you would see if anything was stolen!"

Romeo gave her a wicked smile before slowly approaching.

Ashley shook her head and stepped back.

"Baby, if you are jealous, you just have to say so. I would drop all of them for you and make an honest woman out of you," drawled Romeo, flashing her his dimple.

Ashley hid her grin and stepped forward and up onto the lower step, grabbing him by the collar and pulling him down to her eye level. She bit back a laugh at the look of shock on his face, forcing herself to look serious.

"Why didn't you say so, sweetie pie? I have been dying to lick that dimple of yours for years. I lie awake at night dreaming of the many ways I can make you say my name, drawing it out till the last syl-la-ble.," whispered Ashley seductively, licking her lips.

Romeo swallowed nervously, sweat forming on his forehead. Ashley leaned in towards his dimple and at the last second moved past his cheek and whispered in his ear.

"That is how you seduce someone." Ashley let Romeo go and burst out laughing, at the flabbergasted look on his face. He glared at her and straightened his shirt collar.

"I will get you back for that, Ash. Never taunt a guy like that," groaned Romeo with a shake of the head. Ashley was about to reply when their radio called in an accident. Romeo picked up the radio, and Ashley shut the ambulance doors and jumped in the passenger seat, catching the end of the call.

Gabe stood on the sidewalk, wiping grime and sweat from his forehead. It was still morning, and he was already overheating. He looked into his trolley, wishing that he had washed his thinner shirt the other day. The summer sun beat down on him, his tan skin darkening naturally from overexposure. He scratched at his thick beard, realising he needed to gather some money to buy razors. He pushed his trolley forward, the radio playing softly in the background. Gabe was used to the stares,; most people thought he was crazy, if only that were true. The trolley had a loose wheel, causing it to spin in circles. Gabe forced the trolley forward as he made his way down the road.Gabe forced the trolley forward as he made his way down the road.

He spotted a mostly empty bench and sat down, taking out the half loaf of bread he had found earlier. Gabe pulled off a chunk of bread, chewing slowly. He heard a soft groan and turned sideways to the college student sitting next to him. The kid gave him a disgusted look before getting up from the bench, tossing Gabe his half-eaten egg sandwich and stepping into the street. After that, everything happened in slow motion; a hooter sounded, followed by the sound of tires screeching before impact. Gabe heard the impact of the car hitting the young man and squeezed his eyes shut in preparation for the sight ahead of him. He slowly opened his eyes and took in the scene in front of him. The college student lay in the middle of the road, a few feet from the car, as blood pooled around him. A crowd of people slowly formed a circle, some calling for help on their cell phones. The driver of the car, who looked no older than the student he had hit, broke off in a terrified run away from the scene. Gabe stared at the blood forming on the ground around the boy and stood up. He looked down at the half-eaten sandwich in his hand and took a bite before turning and grabbing the handles of his trolley, ignoring the frantic screams of onlookers. He turned once more to look at the kid, instantly regretting it. The kid looked straight at him with frightened eyes, blood dribbling out of the corner of his mouth.

"Help me," choked the boy, his fingers twitching.

Gabe closed his eyes once more and took a deep breath. He looked down at his trolley and dumped the sandwich among his other items before letting go of the handle.

He stepped into the crowded street, pushing people aside before crouching down next to the boy. One of the onlookers stepped forward, but one look at Gabe's expression stopped him.

"You shouldn't touch him," he shouted.

"Help is on the way," cried another.

"I am the help," answered Gabe, ripping the boy's shirt down the middle.

The boy lifted a bloody hand and grabbed onto Gabe's wrist. Gabe looked down at the blood on his arm and swallowed past the nausea churning in his stomach.

"Don't let me die," pleaded the boy, coughing and choking on his own blood.

Gabe gently touched the boy's ribs, causing the boy to let out an agonizing scream as his body writhed in pain.

"He has a few broken ribs.," stated Gabe.

"Who are you talking to, mister?"

"Myself," replied Gabe. The boy coughed up more blood, suddenly grabbing onto his throat and gasping for breath, his eyes widening in shock.

"He can't breathe!" sobbed someone.

"I think I hear sirens coming."

"They won't make it in time,; he has a collapsed lung and is suffocating. Someone give me a ball point pen," said Gabe.

He took out his pocket knife and flipped it open, waiting for a pen to be handed to him. He bit onto the top and pulled out the ink, making it hollow. Gabe turned to look at the boy and gently felt for the right spot directly between his second and third rib. He took the knife and made a precise small incision, pulling the skin apart and jabbing the pen inside. He waited a second before air escaped out of the pen, the boy opening his mouth and taking a deep breath. Gabe covered the end with each inhale, his own heart rate slowing down.

"He is breathing!" cried a lady as the crowd cheered.

The sirens grew closer, until they suddenly stopped altogether. Gabe heard people approaching and signalled the guy closest to him to come closer.

"Cover this when he breathes in," whispered Gabe, and with one last look at the boy, got up and left. He grabbed his trolley and made his way down the road, ignoring the slight tremor in his hands.

Ashley knelt down next to the young college student, noticing the pen casing sticking out of his chest while a young man kneeled, holding his finger over it with each inhale. Ashley slowly approached them.

"Who did this?" asked Ashley.

"That guy!" said one of the onlookers, pointing towards a homeless man pushing a trolley down the road.

"The homeless guy? He could have killed him," shouted Ashley, checking his neck for any injuries as she set up a manual breathing mask and with Romeo's help got him on the back board.

"He said he knew what he was doing," answered the guy, letting Ashley take over from him.

Ashley headed to the ambulance, looking down at her newest patient.

"Hi, I know you must be scared right now, but we are here to help you. Could you tell me your name?" asked Ashley.

"Troy," whispered the boy, lifting up the mask to speak.

"Alright, Troy, my name is Ashley, and we will be your ride to the hospital," smiled Ashley, trying to lighten the mood.

"That guy saved me. I looked at him like he was nothing, and he saved me," mumbled Troy just before the machine began beeping, and his eyes rolled back in his head.

"Romeo, what is our ETA (Estimated time of Arrival)? His BP (blood pressure) is dropping, and he is going into shock," shouted Ashley, pumping air into his lungs through the BVM (Bag valve mask)

"Five minutes; just hang in there, Ash," yelled Romeo, taking a sharp corner.

"You will not die, you hear me, Troy. Just keep on fighting. We are almost there," said Ashley, checking his pulse rate.

The ambulance came to a sudden stop, and the back doors flew open, a nurse and doctor slid the gurney out. The nurse took over chest compressions, while the doctor squeezed the bag.

"Hit and run, name is Troy, and he is twenty-years-old. His blood pressure dropped on the way," replied Ashley, getting out of the ambulance.

"And that?" said the doctor, pointing towards the plastic pen shell sticking out of the boy's chest.

"A homeless Angel!" answered Ashley, shutting the ambulance doors behind her. The doctor gave her a weird look before wheeling the boy inside.

Ashley stood and wiped the inside of the ambulance, leaving no traces of blood.

She sniffed the air, the cleaning supplies burning her nose, but above that smell was hot percolated fresh coffee.

"Gimme; gimme," cried Ashley, stretching out her arm behind her back, trying to grab the coffee.

"For this cup, I need a hug," said a familiar male voice. Ashley turned around, surprised to find her younger brother Joel standing there.

"Joel," squealed Ashley. His face broke out into a huge grin, Ashley laughed and jumped out of the ambulance and into his open arms. She wrapped her legs around his waist and kissed him on the cheek, before dropping to the floor and with a reprimanding look slapped him upside the head.

"Ouch," groaned Joel, glaring at her.

She smiled and stole his cup of coffee, sitting down on the back of the open ambulance.

"What are you doing here?" asked Ashley, savouring every sip of the coffee.

Her brother stared at the ground, rubbing the back of his neck like he did when he was nervous about something. Something clicked into place, and Ashley stared at her brother.

"No way, don't tell me that Chad sent you here to talk to me!" cried Ashley with a hysterical laugh.

"We are just worried about you, both of you and dad, and we want to be a family again," answered Joel.

"Tell that to dad, actually don't. I am happy to see you and Chad anytime, even mom if she wants. But don't make me go see him," stated Ashley stubbornly.

Her brother turned and leaned against the ambulance next to her and grabbed his coffee back, taking a sip.

"I might be the youngest Ash, but I know things, and I know dad hurt you, and it must have been bad to make you leave your home. But you need to forgive him. He hasn't been himself since you left, and it is making his health worse." "

No, you don't get to guilt me into visiting him. It has been three years. He could have come to visit me. The minute I walked out of that door, I vowed never to go back.

If you knew why, you wouldn't want me to. "

"Then tell me why?" pleaded Joel.

Ashley wanted to tell her brother, if only to have his support. But she had kept this secret for so long, and it would only do more harm. Her brother's loved their dad and saw him as a hero, as he had once been hers. But he was a man just like many others in the world, and he had failed her when she had needed him most. She might hate him, but she would never want her brothers to hate him like she did. No man deserved to die alone without his family there.

"I can't do that, Joel, just go home."

"And what do I tell them?" asked Joel.

"Tell them you couldn't find me or something, please Joel do this for me," begged Ashley.

She knew she was close to tears; her brother searched her face, seeing that she was not going to tell him more and sighed.

"I miss you, Ash," sighed Joel; kissing her on the head.

"I miss me also," whispered Ash.

CHAPTER 2

G abe stood in the darkened alleyway, hidden by the shadows. This was when he felt most calm, barely visible to others. Most people fear the dark, but for Gabe, it was the only time he felt like himself. He stared straight ahead at the building across the street, rubbing his cold fingers together for warmth. The door opened and closed a few times, with couples leaving and entering over the next twenty minutes. He pulled the edges of his brown jacket closer together. Gabe took a step forward just as the door opened, and a woman exited the building. He sucked in a deep breath and quickly slipped back into the shadows. In his rush, he accidentally stepped on a street cat's tail, causing it to scream loudly in the otherwise quiet evening. Gabe swore softly, grabbing onto the industrial-sized dumpster for support. He heard approaching footsteps and made himself appear smaller, standing against the wall, between the gap in the dumpster.

"Is someone out there?" called the woman.

He watched her every movement; she was younger than him, with curly black hair and chocolate brown eyes. Her eyes scanned the area for anything out of the ordinary, and Gabe stood as still as possible.

He watched her shiver slightly, with her arms wrapped around her slender waist. The door behind her opened, and a man stepped out, with a toddler in his arms.

"Hey, babe, what is taking you so long?" asked her husband, putting an arm around her shoulder.

"Sorry, I thought I heard something," shivered the woman.

"Mommy," cried the little girl in her father's arms, holding her arms out for her mother to take her.

"It must have just been a cat," answered the woman with a sigh.

"You have to stop doing this; he is gone," whispered her husband.

"I know that, but I made a promise to myself that I wouldn't give up," cried the woman, taking her daughter into her arms.

She waited for her husband to open the door and followed him back inside.

Gabe let out the deep breath he had been holding, his body slumped with relief. He waited a few more seconds, before crossing the street. He walked up to the intercoms and slid his finger along the names, stopping at the one that meant everything to him. The door opened behind him, causing him to tense up.

"Sorry, are you here to see someone? My daughter dropped her blanket, and I had to come get it," said that familiar feminine voice, that hadn't been directed at him in three years.

Gabe dropped his head, pulling his collar up in the hope of hiding his face. He refused to look at the woman, instead staring at his torn shoes with holes in them.

"I think you should go," replied the woman nervously, he never replied nor made a move to leave.

Gabe just wanted one more look but knew that it would mean disaster. He took a step forward. But a soft, small hand grabbed onto his sleeve, stopping him from moving further.

"Wait! Where did you get this jacket? This was my brother Gabe's," cried the woman, trying to force him to face her.

Gabe slowly turned around, her eyes widening in shock at the recognition of her brother.

22

"Gabe, is that you?" whispered the woman, tears forming in her eyes.

"Gabe died a long time ago, Andy," replied Gabe gruffly, choking on his own emotions.

"Please, just come inside," pleaded Andy, pointing to the door.

The door opened behind them, and her husband popped his head out.

"Andy, are you coming? Gabriella is crying for you," called her husband.

She turned to look at her husband, trying to form the right words but instead opting to show him. She turned back around to find herself alone in the street. Andy searched the area, but there was no one there. She turned to face her husband. Her husband saw her face and instantly knew that something was wrong. He pulled her into his protective arms to comfort her.

"What is it, sweetie? Did that homeless guy say something?" soothed her husband.

"It wasn't a homeless guy; it was my brother," whispered Andy.

Gabe walked straight down the street, refusing to look back. He missed her so much, that sometimes he wished he could just go home. But to her and everyone else he had once known, he was supposedly missing at sea or presumed dead. He liked it that way, but seeing his sister cry for him made him wonder about his choices in the last three years. He had heard the gossip that had been spread around town, about how Dr. Gabriel Bennett had vanished shortly after killing a patient and how he was so riddled with guilt, he killed himself. For all purposes, he was dead, but to the homeless around him, his people, he was 'Angel Gabriel.' He slipped down an alleyway and through a hole in the metal fence, making his way towards his trolley. He kept his eyes cast down, not wanting to attract any unwanted attention from drug sellers or prostitutes. But a loud, piercing scream startled him and forced him to lift his head up in search of the cries. Usually, he would just keep on walking; women screamed often enough in this part of the world, and getting involved could end badly. But the screams sounded different this time, like she was in pain.

Seeing his sister earlier had shaken him more than he thought possible, and to think that it could just as easily be her screaming. That thought alone propelled him forward to make his way towards the agonizing noise. He turned the corner, his eyes taking in the scene ahead of him. A young woman who looked like she was still in her teens, maybe on the brink of adulthood, sat against the side of the dumpster with her knees drawn up and legs wide open. Her hand made small circular rubbing motions and soothing circles over her protruding stomach. Another painful contraction rippled through her small body, causing her body to bend back with the force of pain. Gabe knew that she was either a prostitute or a child slave, left here to die while giving birth to an unwanted child. He could just walk away and not look back, leaving her to have her baby on her own. But she was someone's daughter, and she was alone in a dirty alley, about to have a baby.

He coughed loudly to make his presence known. The girl's blue eyes turned to his face, fear eminent in her eyes as yet another contraction forced her lower half off the ground.

"My name is Gabe, and I might not look like it, but I am a doctor, and I just want to help you," whispered Gabe, walking towards her.

"Baby coming," she said in broken English.

"I know, may I take a look?" asked Gabe, squatting down in front of her.

"Yes," nodded the girl, her black hair drenched with sweat. Gabe slowly lifted her skirt and hid his wince. There was a lot of blood, and if he didn't do something soon, she would die.

What concerned him more was the fact that the baby's foot was sticking out and not its head.

"What is wrong?" "Your baby is the wrong way, and it will tear you up to have him this way," answered Gabe honestly.

Her eyes widened in fear as tears ran down her cheeks.

"Save my baby," sobbed the girl, grabbing his wrist tightly.

Gabe nodded his head and stood up, he took off his belt and handed it to her.

"Bite onto this; it is going to hurt a lot," warned Gabe.

She nodded her head and stuck the leather belt into her mouth. Gabe swallowed and touched the baby's foot. Ten minutes later, Gabe sat on the floor in the dirty alley, staring into the face of a beautiful little girl. The young mother slowly opened her eyes, after passing out from pain.

"My baby!" croaked the girl weakly.

"A little girl, but you need a doctor," said Gabe, slowly getting up.

"Let me see." Gabe knelt down next to her, letting her see her baby.

Her eyes widened in shock as she pushed his hands away and refused to look at the baby.

"No, no! It is not my baby. It is sick and wrong," cried the girl.

"Yes, she is your baby, and she is perfect."

"You call that perfect; she has weird eyes and funny feet," sobbed the girl.

"She has something called Down syndrome, but she is perfectly healthy otherwise. You need to take her and get help!" answered Gabe.

"No! She is sick, and she is a disease! Take her away!" screamed the girl hysterically.

"She is your daughter," stated Gabe.

"No, she is the man that raped me daughter, take it with you, or I will leave it for rats," yelled the girl, her face going pale.

Gabe looked down at the baby, staring back at him with sleepy eyes.

If he left her here, she would leave the baby to die. He looked at the woman once more and walked away with the baby in his arms.

He walked towards the closest restroom and filled the sink with warm water, slowly wiping down the messy baby. The little girl opened her mouth and started crying at the first touch of water. Gabe wrapped her in his arms, rocking her side to side. He made his way out of the bathroom and towards an all-night 24/7 shop. The baby in his arms, started to cry louder and louder with each step he took in the otherwise silent night.

He took out the last of his money and walked into the store, ignoring the looks he got from other people because of the screaming baby in his arms. He bought disposable diapers, powdered baby formula, and a bottle. He paid for it and poured hot water from a coffee machine into the bottle before adding the formula. He then walked towards a park bench and sat down in the cool night air, quickly placing the screaming new-born into a diaper and feeding it the cooling formula. She struggled at first to suckle, finally getting the hang of it. Gabe burped her and rocked her to sleep before standing up. He placed her against his chest, under his top, and walked back towards his trolley.

Ashley felt physically and mentally exhausted; she had barely slept last night with memories assaulting her left and right. She knew she had black bags under her eyes, and that no amount of make-up would hide it. She yawned and climbed into the passenger side of the ambulance.

"Morning, little lady, looks like someone had less sleep than I did," said Romeo smugly.

"My brothers want me to go home to see my dad; he is very sick at the moment," recited Ashley.

"Why haven't you told them what happened?" asked Romeo.

"I don't want them to hate my dad like I do," replied Ashley.

Romeo was about to reply when Chris popped his head through the window.

"Hey, the other paramedics are going out for drinks after work tonight; you want to join us?" inquired Chris.

"Sure, what time?" replied Romeo.

"We are meeting at seven o 'clock at the Lucky Charms, and you, Ash, do you want to join?"

"I will see how my shift goes, but thanks for the invite."
"Spoilsport," teased Chris with a cheeky grin.

The radio interrupted any further chatter with a call coming from an abandoned building.

"Probably a junkie looking for a fix," said Romeo, starting the ambulance.

They drove with the lights flashing, towards the abandoned warehouse, passing cars on the busy highway. They stopped the car in the empty parking lot, and Romeo got out first, Ashley following behind. They shielded their eyes with their hands and stared at the building ahead of them; it looked abandoned and old. Ashley slung her medical bag over her shoulder and followed Romeo into the building. They did a thorough sweep of the clearly empty building, frustrated at the waste of time.

"Must be prank callers," called Romeo walking out of the building.

Ashley followed him out of the building, her eyes landing on the ambulance and grabbing onto Romeo's arm to stop him from moving. The locked back doors were wide open.

"Didn't you lock it?" cried Ashley.

"Yes, I am sure I did. I am too scared to look," mumbled Romeo nervously. They took a step forward, a small whimper coming from inside the van.

"Did you hear that?" asked Ashley, searching the empty parking lot. It was louder this time, filling the silent parking lot.

"That is a baby," cried Ashley running towards the van.

She moved around the open doors, looking inside at a little new-born baby lying on the bed in just a diaper. Ashley bent down and picked the baby up, doing a thorough check-up quickly. The baby looked healthy for a Down syndrome baby. Ashley made soothing noises to the baby as she rocked it back and forth.

"Here is a note and another metal flower," said Romeo, picking it up and reading it out loud.

'Dear EMT,

I apologize for making a false call, but I needed you to come here alone. I helped a young teen deliver her baby last night, and after seeing her differences, the mother wanted nothing more to do with her. I didn't know what else to do with her, so I brought her to you. Sorry for breaking in, and thanks for the morphine.'

27

Romeo chuckled and crumpled the note into a ball, throwing it over his shoulder.

"He has got guts, I will give him that," said Romeo.

"I think I know who it is," answered Ashley, climbing into the back with the baby in her arms.

"And you aren't going to tell me, are you?"

"Nope, not until get all the morphine back."

"Like that would happen.," stated Romeo, peering over his shoulder at her.

"Just please be careful."

"I am always careful," replied Ashley, running a finger along the baby's cheek.

After getting the baby girl checked by a doctor, she sat in the nursery with the little girl in her arms and waited for social services to arrive. She rocked back and forth, the little girl staring at her with big eyes as she sucked on the pink pacifier; Ashley smiled and touched the black hair on top of her head.

"You have had a rough start in life, little one, and it only gets rougher from here. You deserve someone to love you and care for you," whispered Ashley.

The baby yawned around her pacifier in her mouth and closed her eyes.

"Some people don't see beauty when it comes to you. I think you are a gift from God to show us that even imperfection can look beautiful."

She waited for the social services to arrive and handed the baby over to the older lady. Ashley stared down at the baby strapped in the special carrier.

"What are her chances?" asked Ashley.

"Honestly, not that great compared to the other children. But she will go to a special home that handles children like her when she is a bit older," answered the lady.

"Let me know what happens to her, please," pleaded Ashley, handing the lady her number.

"I can see she is a special one," smiled the lady, walking away with the baby.

Ashley walked out of the nursery and made her way down to the cafeteria. She bought herself a cheese sandwich and sat down in the corner by herself. She sat staring out the window, thinking about the thief who had brought her a baby. She remembered the tube sticking out of the boy they had found in the road and the guy with the brown coat that was walking away. Then today as they drove off, she saw him walking down the street again. He was different in some way; she wasn't sure how, but he wasn't like the others. She couldn't be sure, but she wanted to believe that he wasn't a junkie and that the morphine was being used for something important.

Maybe in some ways she was still naive, or maybe she still believed in humanity. She heard footsteps approaching and looked up to see her friend and head Nurse Karla approaching with a tray of food. Karla was the same age as her, with olive skin and blue eyes that matched her short curly brown hair.

"Hey, I heard you brought a baby in today," said Karla, sitting down across from her.

"Yeah, services just took her." "And the mom?" questioned Karla.

Ashley wanted to tell her about the mystery man, but she also wanted to keep it a secret for just a bit longer.

"Gone," answered Ashley, crumbling up her paper from her sandwich.

"Girl, we need to go out tonight and get ourselves a man," said Karla, changing the subject.

Ashley pulled a face, and Karla rolled her eyes.

"And what about Todd?"

"He was in bed with his secretary. Couldn't he be more creative?" laughed Karla, clearly over the guy.

"I don't feel like dressing up and looking all pretty for some drunken guy," pouted Ashley with a swift change of subject.

"First, there is no dressing up to look pretty. Girl, you have thick blonde hair most girls drool over and gorgeous green eyes. If I was into girls, I would so be into you, and those lips of yours are meant for kissing, and those long legs could run a marathon."

"Are you trying to get me in your bed?" teased Ashley.

"I wish, but I only have eyes for things you don't have."

Ashley burst into laughter, her stomach cramping from laughing so hard.

"What is the second thing?" asked Ashley, dabbing her eyes with a tissue.

"You need a man to take care of you, and he might be drunk when you meet, but in the morning, he is all sober,"

Ashley gave her a look and stood up.

"I have to go back to work, and honey, a man should be good sober and drunk," smiled Ashley as she walked away.

Ashley walked into her apartment after her shift, throwing her jacket onto a nearby chair and getting a bottle of cold water out of the refrigerator. She guzzled down most of the bottle and sat down on the stool. It was still light outside, and she had some unwanted energy to burn. She walked into her messy bedroom and threw on her jogging clothing. She put her favourite song on and left her apartment. She jogged in the opposite direction of what she usually did, starting out slow and gaining speed as she went. Ashley loved to look around the neighbourhood, as she watched families settle in for the night. She loved to just watch the children packing up their outside toys and putting away their bicycles and the fathers walking through the door with their briefcase in hand. She loved the simplicity of it all; some would call it boring, but to her, it would be heaven. Ashley made her way through the park tonight, spotting some children having a late swing with their fathers and others getting an ice-cream before supper. She stopped near the pond, out of breath and exhausted. She turned to face the water, watching a group of ducks swim by. She took everything in, her mind drifting with the motion of the water. The sound of trolley wheels on gravel not far from her, pulled her out of her thoughts. She spun around in time to see the tail end of a brown coat turning the corner near the restrooms. Ashley took off on a sprint towards the toilets, wanting to get a better look at her mystery man. She took a short cut across the grass and made her way to the toilets. Darkness descended around them, as the sun hid behind a building.

Ashley turned the corner, searching the area for him. She was growing frustrated with his sudden disappearances all the time. Ashley stood with her back towards the building, planting her hands on her hips.

"Why are you following me?" asked a male voice from the shadows behind her. Ashley spun around, seeing nothing but shadows.

"I want to know who you are and why you are everywhere?" said Ashley.

"Why do you care? I am just a homeless guy with a trolley," replied Gabe.

"We both know you are more than that; just let me talk to you face to face."

"No, go home where it is safe. This isn't your world."

"And it is yours? I see through your act. You might be homeless, but you aren't stupid. Besides, you have been taking my morphine."

"I know."

"Why?"

"It's getting dark; you should go home," said Gabe, turning to leave.

"Wait, please," yelled Ashley, running after his retreating form.

Ashley followed behind him, keeping her distance as to not startle him. Shadows passed over the walls, causing her imagination to run. Ashley hugged her waist as she shivered slightly. She shivered more from the fact that she was alone down a dark alley than from the cool temperature. Her battery on her iPod had died a few minutes earlier, leaving her in total silence. They were close to the bridge near the center of town now; he had to know she was following, but he acted as if nothing out of the ordinary was going on. He turned down an alley, and she followed after him. Suddenly he was gone, leaving her in the alleyway alone. Ashley stood there, contemplating her next move, when two men stepped out from the shadows, both looking less than friendly as they whistled in appreciation. The one had a knife in his hands, and the other a bat. She peered over her shoulder, at the retreating light.

"Lookie here, a stray," said the first guy, licking his lips.

"Are you lost, little girl? This is no place for someone like you," added the second, as he flicked his blade open,

"I was just leaving." replied Ashley.

"And why would you do that? We were just about to have some fun," cackled the second guy, advancing on her.

Ashley screamed loudly and ran down the alley, hearing their footsteps echo directly behind her.

CHAPTER 3

G abe smiled triumphantly; he had lost her. Hopefully, she would just go home and forget all about him. Not that it was likely. He slowed down his pace, looking up at the clear evening sky, stars glittering above. He heard a loud, piercing scream fill the silent air, knowing that his paramedic was in trouble. Gabe turned around and ran straight towards the sound. He skidded to a halt at the entrance to the alleyway, shielding himself in the shadows. Gabe knew this alley like the back of his hand, and knowing it meant that if he just stretched his hand sideways, he would encounter a door. His fingers touched cool metal, and he sighed in relief, praying it was unlocked. The latch clicked, and the door opened slightly. Gabe turned back to the scene in front of him, waiting for the right moment. As she passed by, he grabbed her and pulled her towards him. She refused to go silently, kicking and screaming. Gabe tightened his grip, the two men closing in.

"Shut up and stop fighting me. I can't save your life if you get us both caught," growled Gabe, pulling her flush against his body.

She instantly stopped fighting, her body slumping against his in relief. He pulled open the door and slipped inside with her.

Gabe held her close in one arm and then closed the door with the other. The only sounds coming from the dark room they were in, were the sounds of their laboured breathing. They heard footsteps right outside the door, followed by loud voices.

"Where did she go?"

"She couldn't have just disappeared!"

"Well, she isn't here now." Gabe rolled his eyes, keeping a firm hand on the handle.

It rattled for a few seconds, as someone tried to open it. He pulled it tighter towards him, holding his breath.

"Maybe she is a ghost?"

"Don't be stupid! There is no such thing as ghosts."

Gabe heard a small giggle coming from beside him and tried to give her a reprimanding look in the dark. Once the voices disappeared, Gabe let go of the handle and turned to face her. He looked both ways and headed towards the right, pulling her along.

"Come on, it is this way," said Gabe.

"Where are we?" whispered Ashley, her hand trembling in his.

He rubbed her gently over the soft spot on her inner wrist.

"You will see," said Gabe with a knowing grin.

He pulled the curtain aside, loud music filling the air, and stepped into the room.

Her mouth hung open in shock, and Gabe looked at her and chuckled. He had hidden in here the first time he had nearly been caught by dangerous men.

"We are in a strip club!" cried Ashley, staring at the girls dancing on the stage in scraps of material.

"I thought you might like it," replied Gabe with a devilish grin.

Ashley glared at him, turning to face the exit.

"Let's just get out of here," stated Ashley, feeling totally underdressed in her sweaty sports clothing.

The men were paying to see these women naked, and here she was looking a mess, and half-naked herself in an unflattering way. Her tight shorts showed off her long legs, and her black vest top stopped just above her belly button. Gabe rolled his eyes at her discomfort, grabbing her hand again and pulling her towards the exit.

Ashley wrapped her free arm around her waist, covering her exposed stomach. The bouncer gave them an odd look, letting them go without a word. They stepped out of the stuffy place into the cool night air, scanning the dimly lit parking lot. Gabe let go of her arm and stepped away from her. She stared back at the man who had become such a mystery to her; he was actually a lot younger than she had first thought. He looked to be a few years older than her under that beard and long hair. He crossed his arms and stared right back, trying to intimidate her into submission. But Ashley hadn't made it out there alone by cowering in fear; she crossed her own arms and stared him down. After a few terse seconds, she relaxed her stance.

"Thank you for saving me," said Ashley with a wave of her hand to emphasize where they were.

"Go home," grunted Gabe.

"This isn't the right place for you." Ashley laughed at that comment, tears pouring out of her eyes.

She stopped laughing and wiped her eyes at his confused expression. Ashley sighed and crossed her arms again.

"What is your name?" asked Ashley.

"Gabe."

"That is it? Just Gabe? My name is Ashley James; as a normal person, I have a surname."

He smiled at her witty comment, then turned to leave.

"Wait!" called Ashley nervously.

"Please, could you walk me home? It is quite dark out here, and I am worried those guys will find me again."

"Aren't you worried that I will know where you live and steal from you?"

"No, besides, there isn't much to steal but ladies' clothes, unless you have a thing for them," asked Ashley in a teasing tone.

He arched his brow at her remark and waited for her to point the way back home.

"A man of few words," She sighed in clear frustration that she wouldn't be getting more out of him, and started off in the opposite direction from the alley. They walked in silence, listening to the sounds of traffic and crickets around them.

It wasn't a far walk, and a lot of people were still out at this time of night.

Ashley stopped in front of her apartment, turning to face her hero.

"Why are you living on the streets? I know you are smarter than most people," said Ashley.

"Maybe I am where I want to be."

"And family?"

"I would rather them think I was dead," stated Gabe with a bitter laugh. "Go inside, Ashley, go back to your world and forget I ever existed."

"I can't do that, Gabe; you are a contradiction, an enigma. On the one hand, you are a thief, and on the other, you delivered a baby girl to me after you took care of her."

He turned his back on her, staring at the building across the way.

"Sometimes puzzles are missing pieces, and what is the point of building a puzzle, if it will always be incomplete?"

"Because sometimes the pieces are there, and if you wait till the end, you find them," answered Ashley, opening her apartment door with one last look at Gabe.

Ashley climbed the stairs to the second floor and opened her front door; she slammed it shut behind her. Sinking to the floor with her back against the door, her limbs shook from adrenaline and shock. Tonight had been wild and crazy. She couldn't even bear to think what would have happened if Gabe hadn't rescued her. She knocked her head back against the door repeatedly at her stupidity and stood up with a groan. Ashley put her phone on charge and ran the water for a large and much-needed bubble bath. Tomorrow she would wake up with sore muscles, maybe even a bruise or two. She climbed into the bath with a loud groan, her muscles tensing. She laid her head back and closed her eyes, humming a tune under her breath. The one thing she loved about this apartment was its large bath and shower; she loved to just soak after a long run. Ashley blocked all thoughts from her mind, dozing off. The sound of her cell phone ringing in the distance, caused her to wake up.

She jumped out of the bath, trying not to slip on the wet floor, and half-wrapped a towel around her wet body as she ran towards her cell phone. She grabbed it and pushed answer without looking at the caller I.D. At the sound of the other voice on the other side, she instantly regretted not looking beforehand. The one voice she never thought to hear again, the one that haunted her still even after three years, was on her phone right now. Ashley fought off the nausea rising in her belly and tried to keep her breathing steady.

"Hello, Ash, I hope you don't mind me calling? But Joel gave me your number. When I heard that they wanted you to come back home, I knew I had to help," said Reed Silverstone.

Ashley gritted her teeth, staring at her reflection in the mirror across the way.

"You don't have to worry, Reed; no one but my dad knows, and he doesn't believe me. So don't waste your breath; I am never coming home," replied Ashley, her body breaking out in a cold sweat.

"Ashley, Ashley," tittered Reed.

"You have it all wrong; I want you to come home."

She nearly dropped the phone at that declaration; it was the last thing she expected him to say.

"You do?" whispered Ashley.

"Of course, I told your father that I was still willing to marry you, and he agreed. He told me that he was sorry for the way you acted and hopes that he will be alive to see his first grandchild."

"I will never marry you, Reed; just saying your name makes me sick. I will never go home, so go find someone else," shouted Ashley.

"I would, but it seems that people are starting to talk, saying that I must have done something to make you leave. Now, darling, we both know you just over reacted, and if you would just consider my offer," drawled Reed.

"If you think that, then you are seriously sick in the head, and for my dad, I hope you both rot together in that small town," screamed Ashley, slamming her phone down onto the table.

Ashley stood staring at her reflection in the mirror, tears running down her cheeks. What was becoming of her life? She thought she was over it all.

She wiped her eyes dry and climbed onto the bed, still, with the towel around her, and cried herself to sleep.

Gabe stood outside her apartment to make sure that she was alright; he waited until the light went off before leaving. He took a slow stroll down the road, back to where he had hidden his trolley. The wind blew, and a small piece of paper flew and landed on his chest. Gabe lifted it off and was about to crumple it into a ball when he recognized the picture. He turned it over to look at it clearly. The photo was of him and his sister Andy at his graduation with their parents. Gabe clutched the photo in his hand and ran towards where his trolley was being kept. The sheet of cardboard covering it was lying aside, and the trolley was gone. Everything inside was laying scattered across the ground. Gabe dropped to his knees, frantically scooping up the photo's lying outside the albums in a puddle of dirty water.

"No! No! No!" cried Gabe, shaking water loose from the albums.

A few albums were left still dry and undamaged. He gathered them into his arms, stumbling to his feet and sat down on an overturned crate. Gabe opened the first one, the photo ink smudged and ruined. A tear drop landed onto the page. He hurriedly wiped his eyes with the back of his hand and went through the rest of the album. He left the albums on the crate and stood up, kicking the empty box across the alley. This was everything that meant something to him, and it was ruined. He slammed his fist into the wall, yelling in pain. Gabe stood there, hugging his bruised hand to his chest and heaving angrily. He snatched the albums up into his arms and strode off with them. He needed to keep them safe before he lost them for good. His hand throbbed consistently, but he ignored it as he walked into the night with all that was important to him.

Gabe stopped outside the now-familiar apartments and pushed the right button. "Hello? Hello?" called his sister Andy. He fought the urge to reply, wanting to talk to her and hug her so much. But he wasn't her brother anymore. He leaned his forehead against the intercom, listening to her say hello repeatedly.

"I am coming down, and you better be gone if this is a prank," yelled Andy.

Gabe smiled ruefully and placed the stack of undamaged albums on the top step; he crossed the road and stood in the shadows watching. His sister stepped outside with an annoyed expression on her face, until she looked down at the albums lying there, and her expression changed to one of confusion then sudden understanding. Andy bent down and picked them up, turning to search the empty streets.

"Gabe! I know you are out there. Please just come home to us," pleaded Andy.

Her eyes searching for any signs of him, he stood still as a statue. Her shoulders slumped in defeat as she went back inside. Gabe swallowed past the lump in his throat and walked away.

Two weeks had passed since she had last seen Gabe; she fought against the constant pull to go find him. But thoughts of those dangerous men in the alley put all stops to any further plans of finding him. She had thrown herself into her work the last few weeks, falling into bed exhausted at night only to start over again the next day. Today had been gruelling, and the day had barely begun; she was counting the hours until she could go home. She looked over at Romeo, who was in an exceptionally good mood, causing her mood to worsen. He just flashed her, his dimpled smile and tweaked a strand of her hair. Annoyed, she swatted his hand away, pouting as he chuckled in return. They were just finishing a routine call for an allergic reaction; some child had eaten something they weren't supposed to and had swelled up to the size of a balloon. But they had arrived in time to save the child, and the child was currently asleep in bed at the moment. They stood on the pavement outside the modest-sized house, and waved once more to the grateful mother. Ashley turned to face the ambulance and just stopped herself from screaming out loud at the sight of someone leaning against the side. Ever since her call from Reed, she had been extra jumpy,every shadow scaring her. She forced herself to relax and approached Gabe;

He had shaved a lot of his beard off and looked almost handsome with that long hair of his. He stood with his back against the truck with his ankles crossed.

"And to what do I owe this pleasure?" asked Ashley sarcastically.

Her nerves were strung high, and sarcasm was her best defense, especially when it came to this man.

"I need some more morphine and figured that I should ask instead of taking," answered Gabe with a careless shrug.

"And what? You thought I would just give it to you?"

"Nope," said Gabe with an emphasis on the letter P, with a devilish grin.

"But it was worth a try."

Romeo approached them with a critical eye, Gabe nodded his head in greeting. He turned to look at Ashley again, pushing himself off the side of the ambulance.

"See you around, Ashley."

Ashley bit her lip as she watched him saunter down the road; there was no other word to describe the way he walked. She turned to look at Romeo and rolled her eyes at his protective gaze.

"Wait! What do you need it for?" called Ashley at the last second.

He peered over his shoulder to flash her one last smile and carried on down the road, with his hands in his coat pockets, and no trolley in sight. She stared after him, only turning to face Romeo when he was totally out of sight.

"So that is our thief?" stated Romeo, pulling open the driver-side door.

"Yeah, he is, and he also saved my life."

Romeo stuck his head back out the door and stared at her.

"He did what?"

"Calm down, Romeo, I will explain on the way," said Ashley, climbing into the passenger side.

CHAPTER 4

He knew he was playing with fire, coming back here all the time. But he couldn't stay away. They were his family, she was his only sister, and he loved her. He waited and watched, hoping for a glimpse. About to turn and leave, he saw the door open, and she finally exited her apartment with little Gabriella in her arms. She laughed and turned to look over her shoulder at the other woman walking through the door. He caught sight of the second woman and sucked in a deep breath, as his heart beat faster, at the sight of the one woman who really did wish he was dead. He felt dizzy with the knowledge that she still spoke to his sister, even after what had happened to her husband. He looked down at his shaking hands, and made sure there was no blood on them, before taking a deep breath. It was irrational, but he kept seeing the blood on his hands when he thought of her. But that was all in the past; she was in the past just like his sister. He stared at the two children he had loved as his own, holding onto their mother's hand, and felt his heart constrict. Blood rushed to his head, his ears ringing as dizziness over took him. He needed to get out of here before he was seen.

Gabe walked back down the alley with purpose, tears stinging his eyes, at the life he had thrown away for a single lousy promise. He wiped his wet cheeks on his shoulders, and slid down the dumpster. With his back against it, he stared at the wall in front of him, as far from Andy's place as possible. Suddenly, the clouds above opened up, and rain came down. Gabe just sat in the alley, as the rain soaked him through his clothing to the skin. Why wouldn't the past just leave him alone? He had given up everything, and still, it haunted him. His teeth began to chatter from the cold as his hair plastered to the sides of his face. He needed to forget, for just one night, everything that had happened. He stood up and made his way towards the closest liquor store. He bought a bottle of Jack and sat down on the side of the pavement in the rain, drinking. He smiled to himself as he looked around with blurry eyes. He knocked over the remainder of the bottle and watched it roll down the road. He let out a loud drunken giggle as it stopped under a booted foot. He blinked through his haze clouding his mind, in time to register that the bottle wasn't moving anymore. He looked up at the man towering over him, his expression malicious. Gabe gave him a reassuring smile, or he sure hoped it was one, and waved at the other man standing a few feet behind him.

"Ha! Llooo! Boys," emphasized Gabe.

They looked at each other, then back at him. By the look in their eyes, they were itching for a fight, well so was he.

"Did he just call us boys?" questioned the one towering over him.

"We should go; he looks like a homeless guy. Besides, I heard a squad car earlier on, and this man is so wasted anyway."

"Who you calling wasted?" muttered Gabe, swaying side to side. He leaned back on his hands and looked up at the starry sky.

"The rain is gone," smiled Gabe lopsided.

"He bought the good stuff, man, which means he must have good money even if he looks homeless," said the first guy.

"No.. nope.. no money. I live on the streets right over there," pointed Gabe in what he hoped was the right direction.

"Just give us your wallet, and we will see for ourselves."

"No, it's mine. All I got lef..f...f...t.," said Gabe, staggering to his feet.

He stumbled slightly sideways, pushing through the two boys, as he made his way across the parking lot.

"He can barely walk," whispered the second one.

"Exactly, which means he is an easy target."

Gabe felt someone grab his jacket,; he tried to tug free, but they held fast. He turned and swung his fist forward, hitting into something solid. The boy yelled in pain, stumbling backward.

"I think he broke my nose!" garbled the boy.

"Don't worry; it will stop bleeding sometime," laughed Gabe, shaking his aching fist.

The first guy stepped forward with his fist raised. He got in a few good shots, drunk and all, before they left him lying in a puddle of water on the floor. He groaned in pain, his lip swollen and bleeding, his ribs hurting with each breath he took. Gabe rolled over and knelt onto the pavement, as he vomited. He stood on shaky feet and made his way down the street towards the one place that he knew he could trust. He blinked a few times to see past the haze, his head pounding from more than alcohol, and read the apartment numbers till he found the surname James. He pushed the button, his knees giving way.

"Hello!" said the feminine voice.

"Ashley, I need your help," croaked Gabe, groaning in pain at the pressure on his ribs.

He waited with his finger on the button, realizing that she was probably calling the police on him.

"Alright, I will be right down," replied Ashley before the intercom went dead.

Ashley slipped on her thick black hooded jacket and slid her feet into her fluffy pink slippers, and yanked the front door open. It was close to midnight, and she had been on the verge of falling asleep when the intercom had buzzed. Ashley ran down the two flights of stairs and pulled open the large red door, stepping into the cool night air. She heard a pained groan and turned sideways to find a large figure slumped against a tree by the sidewalk. Ashley ran down the front steps, soaking her slippers on the wet cement.

She knelt down in front of the figure. A street lamp above shone down on them, as she let out a startled gasp at the cuts and bruises on his face. He blinked open his blue eyes, his pupils larger than normal.

"You shouldn't be sleeping; you could have a concussion," whispered Ashley, taking hold of his arm and helping him onto his feet.

He gritted his teeth in pain, sweat running down his face, as he wrapped his free arm around his sore ribs to keep them in place.

"I see your ribs are bruised; just to let you know I live on the second floor," said Ashley.

"Just my luck," grumbled Gabe, grabbing onto the wall to steady himself before they both fell down.

They made it up to the apartment, the pain sobering him instantly. Ashley left him to lean against the wall as she unlocked the front door. Ashley felt a shudder go through her and shook it off before turning to face him. He looked more awake and alert, his face red from the trip up the stairs. He shrugged her hands off and waited by the door until she walked through before following. Ashley pulled off her wet slippers, pulling a face at the sound of them splattering on the ground. She curled her bare toes on the cold wooden floors as she headed to the kitchen. She knew without looking behind her, that he was following her. So she just switched the kettle on and stood with her back against the counter to watch him. He stood in the doorway, leaning against the doorframe.

"What happened?" asked Ashley.

"I got jumped," was his quick reply.

"And you weren't drunk when it happened?" questioned Ashley, as she turned to get the medical kit out from under the sink.

"Yes, but that was beside the point. I don't usually drink; I had a weak moment."

"And look what happened," stated Ashley, motioning towards the chair.

He reluctantly sat down with a grim expression. Ashley stood between his legs and took the piece of cotton wool with disinfectant on and dabbed at the cuts on his face. He barely flinched, staring at her with those intense eyes all the time.

She turned to move away, but he gently grabbed her wrist.

"Thank you," whispered Gabe, rubbing soothing circles on the inner part of her wrist.

"Why did you come here?"

"It was the only place I trusted," answered Gabe honestly.

She nodded in acceptance, and put the kit away, turning to face him once again.

"I am making coffee; you can take a shower and some pain meds. All I can offer you is the two-seater to sleep on."

"I don't intend to stay," replied Gabe, using the table for support to stand up.

"You won't even make it down the stairs; besides, I need to keep an eye on that concussion. Now go take a shower; it's the first door down the hall, and there are fresh towels there." Ashley watched him walk down the hall, her heart stuttering in her chest.

She had just welcomed a homeless guy to spend the night in her house. She sat down in the chair; he had vacated, burying her head in her hands. She hadn't noticed how long she had been sitting like that until he cleared his throat.

Ashley's head shot up, her eyes red from lack of sleep. He stood in the doorway with just a towel around his waist. Her mouth went dry at the sight of him; he was better looking than she had imagined. His black hair was longer than she liked, but he had strong cheek bones and a well-toned body.

"My clothes are soaked," said Gabe, shaking his wet hair side to side.

"Yeah.. uhm.. I think my brother left a pair of sweats here last time," stuttered Ashley, standing up, and nearly knocking the chair over in the process.

He chuckled and stepped aside, letting her squeeze past. Ashley escaped to her room, her cheeks red from embarrassment. She dug through her chest of drawers, finding the large black pants Chad had left here the last time he had stayed over. She walked out of the room and handed him the pants, walking back past him and into the kitchen to make the coffee she had promised him.

Gabe watched her retreat into the kitchen, chuckling under his breath. He liked to see her beautiful face red with embarrassment. When was the last time he had enjoyed a woman's presence this much? It had been years, but the fact remained that she was still too far out of his league. He lived on the streets, while she lived in an apartment. He had lost everything, while she had her whole life ahead of her. He pulled on the sweats, moaning out loud at the softness of the fabric against his bruised flesh. He slipped back out of the bathroom and made his way back to the kitchen where she stood with her back to him, humming a song under her breath.

"They fit," stated Gabe.

He watched her hand shake slightly and her shoulder's tighten with tension. She slowly turned around with two cups of coffee in hand. He walked up to her, seeing the quick flash of fear in her gorgeous green eyes before she masked them and freed her from one of the cups. He stood inches from her, his eyes trained on her over the rim of his cup as he took a sip. He almost groaned out loud after just the first sip. It had been so long since he had a homemade cup of coffee. She averted her eyes, moving past him and into the sitting room. He turned and followed her, as she pointed to the large two-seaters.

"Sorry, this is all I have; my brother actually says it is quite comfortable," stated Ashley with an apologetic shrug.

"It looks heavenly after what I have been sleeping on the last few years."

He watched the different display of emotions cross her features, knowing she was fighting the instinct to ask him questions. He admired and respected her patience and the fact that she didn't pry. He sat down, and a satisfied moan slipped out before he could stop it. He opened his eyes and looked straight at her. She bit her lip, worrying it between her teeth. He smiled and leaned back, closing his eyes again, as he drained the rest of the cup. Gabe lifted his feet up onto the other end and slid sideways a bit. He felt her presence, knowing she was watching him.

"I don't have a concussion, so please go sleep," whispered Gabe, his eyes still closed.

A few seconds later, a warm blanket was draped over him, and the room was thrown into darkness. Gabe rolled over sideways, his ribs protesting at the sudden movement. Sleep slowly claimed him. He was in a deep sleep, dreaming of his family when the sound of terrified screams awoke him. This was becoming a pattern, hearing women screaming around him. He sat up and bit his lip in pain, instantly remembering he was in Ashley's apartment. The room was dark around him; he listened as a much softer cry followed the screams, and he stood up to make his way towards her. A fierce protectiveness rose up inside of him. If someone was in there hurting her, he would be dead in the next five minutes, declared Gabe.

The door was slightly open, and the lamp still on. He popped his head into the room, finding Ashley alone in the room asleep. Confused, he turned to leave when another cry came from her room. He looked back inside at her asleep in the middle of the bed. . She looked young and vulnerable, curled into a ball as she moaned. She rolled over and let out a frightened whimper. Gabe slowly walked towards the bed and sat on the edge, stretching out his hand. Before he made contact, her green eyes flew open, her mouth opening in a silent scream.

"Ashley, it is just me, Gabe. I heard you having a nightmare and came to check on you," said Gabe soothingly.

She seemed to come back to herself, blinking a few times. She let out a startled gasp and pulled the blankets up to cover her. Gabe wasn't sure what to say; he barely saw women cry unless it was because of a death.

"I am sorry if I scared you," whispered Gabe, standing up awkwardly.

She shook her head, her blonde hair falling out of the bun she had tied it in.

"No, it's not you. I am sorry for just crying like this," mumbled Ashley, tears running down her cheeks.

"No, it is fine; I clearly gave you a fright." "Yeah, you actually did, but I was having a nightmare first," answered Ashley. It was on the tip of his tongue to ask her what she had dreamt of.

Then it would mean telling her his secrets in return. He wasn't ready for her to look at him with disgust and hate. Once he told her, it would change everything. He nodded his head and turned to walk out of the room.

"Gabe, thank you," called Ashley.

He swallowed past the lump in his throat and headed back to his makeshift bed; he laid back down and willed sleep to claim him. His thoughts focused on the woman, sleeping a few feet away. Ashley woke up later than usual, extremely grateful that today was her day off.

She felt more relaxed than she had in the last two weeks, even with a stranger in her house. She took a quick shower and pulled on a pair of clean skinny white jeans and a loose black knit jersey. She left her hair loose and made her way to the sitting room, only to find the blankets all folded neatly and the room empty. She pushed down feelings of disappointment and made herself some scrambled eggs for breakfast. Ashley sat by herself eating and thinking about the mysterious guy called Gabe. Afterwards, she took the time to clean her apartment. Once the place was clean, she checked her watch and sighed; it wasn't even lunch time yet, and she was bored. She slipped on her sneakers and got in her old rusted blue Volkswagen and drove over to the social services. She usually didn't do this, but the little girl that she had brought in was still on her mind. She found Jill, the lady that had taken her away and asked about the little baby.

"We named her Melody, and she has grown so much in the last few weeks," said Jill with a fond smile.

"Has anyone showed any interest?" asked Ashley.

"No, she is very special, and it will take a unique couple to want her," replied Jill.

"May I see her?"

"It is nearly time for her feeding; why don't you do the honours?" Ashley's face lit up in excitement, as she followed Jill down the long corridor and into the nursery.

They walked over to a wooden crib in the corner; Ashley peered inside.

She smiled down at the gorgeous little girl smiling back at her.

"Hello Melody, look how big you are getting," cried Ashley as she gently lifted her up into her arms.

She sat in the seat allocated and accepted the bottle from Jill; Melody stared up at her with the same big eyes, her black hair curling a bit.

"Do you know anything about her mom?" asked Jill.

"No, we just found her. But I might know someone who might know," answered Ashley.

She stayed for most of the morning, playing with Melody until the baby fell asleep. Ashley was reluctant to let the girl go, but becoming too attached would just end in disaster. Ashley got into her car and drove towards Romeo's place. She got out of the car and knocked on his door; he opened the door looking like he had just woken up, as he was still in just sleep shorts with bed hair that stuck out all over the place.

"Sorry, did I wake you?" asked Ashley.

"Yes, you did, but if you make me coffee, I will forgive you," teased Romeo, opening the door wider.

Ashley made her way to the kitchen and started the coffee; she turned around and found herself comparing Romeo to Gabe. He stood in the doorway, just like Gabe had, yet she felt nothing but friendship for him.

"You are staring," said Romeo.

"Sorry, I was daydreaming," fibbed Ashley.

"I know I can be a bore, but that just hurts my feelings," teased Romeo, placing his hand over his heart.

"I am just so exhausted; I keep having nightmares, and my family won't stop pestering me to come home. After Reed called, I have been a bit."

"Hang on love, he called you? When?" interrupted Romeo.

"Two weeks ago, he wants to get back together and has my father's permission."

"Yeah, well, he doesn't have mine," said Romeo, walking towards her and pulling her into a hug. Ashley sighed and let him hold her up for a while, her emotions all over the place.

They spent the rest of the afternoon watching movies together and eating popcorn and other junk food. On her way to the door, Romeo grabbed her hand. Ashley turned to face him.

"Call me day or night, no matter what," said Romeo.

"You don't need to worry about me," replied Ashley.

"I will always worry about you," answered Romeo, leaning forward and kissing her on the cheek.

She drove past a pizza place and ordered herself a meaty pizza, then drove home with the tantalizing aroma filling her car. Tomorrow was an early start again, and she just wanted to curl up and sleep after a nice hot bath. She parked the car and grabbed the pizza box, before heading towards the door.

"Hello, Ashley," said a familiar voice from behind her.

The voice startled her, recognition setting in and her veins turning cold. Ashley gripped the pizza box firmly in her hands and turned to face her ex, Reed, the man who had destroyed her relationship with her father. Because of his actions, she had to leave everything and everyone she loved.

"What are you doing here, Reed?" asked Ashley in what she hoped was a calm voice.

"Why did you come to see me?"

"I just came to talk to you," replied Reed.

"I want you to leave! Get in your car and go!"

"I have nothing to say to you. Go, or I will be forced to call the police," Ashley said firmly.

"You wouldn't dare," growled Reed, his eyes simmering with rage.

He stepped forward and grabbed her upper arms in a tight grip, causing Ashley to let out a painful cry. His eyes were filled with coldness that shook her to the core.

"Don't mess with me," declared Reed.

"Let her go!" demanded a stern voice.

Ashley felt herself relax slightly at the fierce demand made by Gabe. She wouldn't even try to wonder why he was here, just that he was.

Ashley felt herself relax slightly at the fierce demand made by Gabe. She wouldn't even try to wonder why he was here, just that he was.

"Stay out of this. This is between us," yelled Reed, shaking her slightly.

"I want you to leave," cried Ashley.

"You heard her. Let her go," said Gabe in a commanding voice, holding onto his own temper by a mere thread of self-control.

"And why would I do that?" asked Reed.

"Because if you don't, I will tell everyone how you tried to rape me," shouted Ashley.

He turned fierce eyes back on her, raising his hand to strike her. Gabe moved faster than she thought possible, grabbing Reed's hand and twisting it behind his back. Reed instantly let her go, crying out in pain. Ashley stumbled backward, looking up, just as her brother, Joel, stepped out from the shadows. By the look on his face, he had heard it all.

CHAPTER 5

Ashley closed her eyes, shutting out the world around her. She took a deep calming breath in and out before opening her eyes and staring straight at Joel. Her usually calm brother looked ready to murder Reed at any moment. She needed to calm things down before it all blew up in her face. Joel turned to look at her, his fists clenched tight.

"Is that true, Ash? Is that why you left home?" asked Joel, through gritted teeth.

"Does Dad know?" Ashley fought the tears trying to break free; her brother was devastated that he hadn't known.

"Joel, please go inside, take the pizza with you, and I will explain in a minute," said Ashley, fighting to stay in control and not break down in front of Reed.

"I will not leave you outside with him!" Joel sneered, a finger pointed straight at Reed.

"Please, Joel, I have my friend Gabe here taking care of it, and I need to talk to Reed and Gabe alone," pleaded Ashley.

He gave her the look that said he was only agreeing for now to keep the peace and that they would talk later.

"Fine! But that doesn't mean I will let it drop when we get back home, Reed!" declared Joel, with one last look of disgust at Reed.

Ashley handed him the cold pizza as he passed her and waited for him to enter the building before turning to face Reed.

"I want you to leave me and my family alone, or I will tell everyone back home what you did. I can't promise that Joel will keep this a secret, and I don't care right now. But this is my home, and if you ever come back, then I won't be liable for my actions."

"You have ruined everything!" screeched Reed, spit flying out of his perfectly white teeth.

"Actually, you did that to yourself when you laid an unwanted hand on her," said Gabe, letting go of his arm that he still had firmly behind Reed's back and pushed him towards his car.

He gave them one last scornful look before getting in the car and driving away. Ashley felt her energy draining out in a rush as she stared down at her sneakers. She was unable to look Gabe in the eyes, now that he knew her secret. Gabe took firm control of the anger he felt towards Reed and stepped towards Ashley. He lifted her chin gently with his fingers, so that she could see the compassion in his eyes, with no hint of judgment.

"What he did was the coward's way of getting what he wanted. You were smart and brave to do what you did. Now go talk to your brother, and I will see you soon," said Gabe, letting his fingers linger on her cheek for a few seconds longer before stepping back.

Ashley found herself nodding her head in agreement, and turning to open the door.

She stopped with the door open, peering over her shoulder to look at Gabe one last time.

"Why were you here anyway?" asked Ashley.

"I came to say thank you for last night and to return your brother's pants. But now isn't a good time, so I will keep them for now," replied Gabe, turning away from her, and walking back into the shadows of dusk he had appeared out of. Ashley made her way slowly up the stairs, thinking of what she would tell her brother.

Her thoughts were a mess, and she wanted to curl in a ball, humiliation and shame washed over her knowing that her brother now knew what Reed had tried to do. She opened the door, stunned silent by her brother pulling her into a hug and crying onto her shoulder. She wrapped her arms around him, making soothing noises as he continued to cry. After a few minutes, he pulled back and wiped his eyes on the sleeves of his shoulders, before pulling her to sit down next to him. He wrapped his arm around her and tucked her close against his body.

"I am so sorry, Ash. I have been so mad at you for the whole Dad thing and for not marrying Reed," started Joel.

"I didn't want you to hate Dad," whispered Ashley.

"Wait! Dad knew, and he let that man walk around town, he chased you away from us!" cried Joel.

"Does Chad know about this?" "Of course not, Joel. I told Dad, and he called me a liar. Said I was taking the coward's way out of being engaged and that he was ashamed of me. I knew you two would believe me, but I didn't want you to get into trouble by doing something stupid and hurting Reed," sobbed Ashley.

He turned her chin up so that she was looking into the same deep green eyes as her own; her younger brother seemed wiser than her at the moment.

"Never keep something like that from us again. Dad was wrong, and I understand if you never want to come home again. But don't shut us out, and besides, Reed deserves to go to jail for what he tried to do."

"Thank you, Joel, for being the best baby brother ever. But I don't want you to be angry at Dad, alright? I am already angry enough for all three of us. Like you said, Dad is sick at the moment, and he needs you and Chad with him."

"And what about his daughter?" asked Joel.

"I shamed him," whispered Ashley.

"No, he did that to himself, and I bet he has made himself sick over this," stated Joel.

"Then why hasn't he asked me to come home or called me in the last three years?" asked Ashley.

"Maybe he is ashamed of his actions and doesn't think he is worthy of you," answered Joel.

"That doesn't make sense, Joel. Reed said that Dad still wants me to marry him still," cried Ashley, throwing her hands in the air in frustration.

"He lied, that is why I came here. Dad told me that Reed had heard we wanted you to come home, and he told me to come here to check up on you. Maybe he has been protecting you all this time, thinking you safer this side where Reed couldn't get near you."

"I can't imagine why he would think that, when there is you and Chad to protect me. Anyways, let's not think about this anymore; my head hurts, and I am exhausted. I just want to enjoy a cold pizza with my brother," answered Ashley, snuggling back against him.

"I am still going to beat the hell out of Reed for touching you," whispered Joel, rubbing over her bruised arm.

He paced back and forth under the bridge, his emotions all over the place. He had never wanted to hurt someone like he had when that guy had touched Ashley. He had seen the bruises that guy had left there, his own self-control threatening to break. He laughed out loud at the mere thought of wanting to take her away from everything bad. Someone like her didn't need someone like him. He needed to stop thinking like this; she wasn't his and never would be. He rubbed his hands over his face, trying to clear his thoughts.

"Angel Gabriel! Angel Gabriel!" yelled a young voice.

Gabe turned around, spotting the nine-year-old boy standing on the other side, under the bridge, calling him.

He slowly approached the boy, feeling guilty that he had forgotten his sole purpose for going to see Ashley. The boy wrapped his thinner than usual arms around Gabe in greeting.

"I thought you hadn't seen me," cried Manuel.

"I always see you, Manny. Now come, let's go see that little sister of yours," replied Gabe.

The boy nodded his head and led the way behind one of the cement pillars. His mother had built them a makeshift shelter from scraps she had found, keeping a draft out at night.

Gabe crouched down and followed Manny inside; the one oil lamp was lighting up the small room. The boy walked over to a large green bucket and took out a partially clean rag, then sat near his five-year-old sister's head as he dabbed her sweaty face.

"Where is your mother?" asked Gabe.

"She is out working again."

Gabe knew what type of work she did, but it wasn't his place to judge. Sometimes you did what you needed to do to survive. He nodded his head and approached the little girl. Her olive skin clammy and pale, her stomach extended slightly.

"How long has Angie been like this?" asked Gabe. "Since this morning."

"And why didn't you call me?"

"I tried to, but I couldn't find you.," cried Manny.

Gabe felt another wave of guilt wash over him; he had been so focused on other stuff that he hadn't been there for the people who needed him.

"Did you get the special medicine to take away her pains?" asked Manny.

"No, I didn't. But they won't work anymore. She has an infection and needs a doctor."

"But you are a doctor, are you not?" "Yes, I am, but she needs a special one that can give her medicine.," answered Gabe.

He lifted her torn yellow shirt up, her stomach red and swollen.

"Manny, we need to get her help or she will die."

"No, you will not take my daughter anywhere!" said a voice behind them.

Gabe turned to face twenty-five-year-old Maria; she was dressed in a short black skirt that barely covered anything and a top that showed off her assets.

"Maria, I know you are scared, but she is very sick and she will die," cried Gabe.

"She is illegal like us, and they will take her and send her back," replied Maria.

"Mama, it hurts," sobbed Angie, her face contorting in pain.

"I know, baby, mama is trying to get you the medicine you need."

Gabe walked out of the tent and pulled Maria aside, making sure the children couldn't hear.

"No medicine will help her; she has an infection, and maybe even her appendix has burst. If she doesn't get operated on, you will be burying her," stated Gabe.

Maria buried her head in her hands, the weight on her small shoulder more than most would be able to handle. She was much too young to be a mother, but she loved her children.

"No! She is my little girl, and she and Manny are all I live for. Please, Señor, you have to help her here.," sobbed Maria.

"I can't help her; she needs a hospital, Maria."

"Take her to the hospital, go with Manny and make her better. But I trust you, Señor, and I want my baby back."

Gabe wasn't sure how he would make that happen, but he would. He nodded his head and crawled back into the little house. He told Manny the plan and lifted the crying girl into his arms. She was much too light for five, his heart breaking for what these children had to live through. He walked out with her cradled in his arms, Manny following beside him with her limp hand in his.

"What will you tell the doctor? So they don't take her away," asked Manny.

"As far as anyone knows, I am your father," stated Gabe.

"Yes, papa," grinned Manny. Gabe carried the little girl to the hospital, not far from where they were. He entered the front doors with Manny still holding her little hand.

"Can we get help here, my daughter is very sick," shouted Gabe.

What looked to be the head nurse ran towards them, signalling for another to follow.

"My girl is very sick; she has a sore tummy, and I think it is her appendix, and she will die without help," cried Gabe.

The nurse showed him where to lay her and lifted up Angie's top.

"Papa, will Angie be alright?" asked Manny, his eyes filling with real tears.

"Sir, we need to take her to surgery right away, stay here and fill out some forms," said the nurse; her look one of concern for his lack of care and that he better have answers.

Gabe stood his ground, placing his hands on Manny's shoulders. He played the part of a devastated father well.

"Please don't let my Angie die," begged Gabe, real concern for the little girl showing.

He had known her for two years now and cared deeply for her and her brother. He took the pen and clipboard and sat down in a plastic chair with Manny seated next to him. He knew they looked a mess, but once Angie was better, they would never be seen again. A few minutes later, the same nurse approached, her name badge said Karla. He looked her straight in the eyes as he told the lie that would save this little girl.

"I know what it looks like, Karla, like she has been neglected, and you are obligated to call social services. But I am a good father, and I love my daughter, I work twelve hours every day to give them food. The last few days I have been working double shifts, and my children were with a friend; they called me today at work and told me that she was sick. I found the friend watching television while my girl lay in bed dying, so when you decide whether or not to call them, then think about that," recited Gabe.

Karla looked back at him with tears in her eyes; she nodded her head and took the forms he had filled in. Gabe found some change in his pocket and bought Manny a packet of chips and a cool drink while they waited. A few hours later, a doctor came out to inform them that Angie would be alright; she was on strong medication and in a few days would be well enough to go home. He told them that she was sleeping and that they could go see her, but they needed to let her rest.

After their quick visit, they left; Gabe carried a sleepy Manny on his back. The boy peeked over his shoulder to see Gabe's face.

"You told a good lie; I almost cried myself," said Manny, giggling.

Gabe bounced him up and down, hearing him groan in pain at the rough treatment.

"That is enough from you; I should have let them take her and you away. Maybe then you would have clothing and a house to live in and go to school."

"But we wouldn't have our mama," said Manny.

"I know that, and I made a promise to your mother. But tomorrow you need to go there and tell Angie to call me papa for now."

"I will do this, but how will you get her home?" asked Manny.

"Leave that to me; now go tell your mama she is doing fine," replied Gabe, putting Manny down.

Gabe walked over to the barrel and stuck his cold fingers over the fire. He knew what he had done was wrong. But he had known Angie and her family for two years, and he couldn't bear for them to be separated. The minute she was out of the hospital, he would find a way to make their life better. Find a way to get Maria out of the life she was in and get those children into a school.

Over the next few days, he searched the scrapyard for items to sell, building a small pile of money with odd jobs around the neighbourhood, and in the evenings, he would go with Manny to visit Angie. Almost a week later, he knew it was time to bring her home. The nurse Karla had told him that she had waited till Angie was fully better, but she had to call social services soon. He told Manny to stay home tonight and walked down to the hospital. Gabe still had his old hospital badge, praying that he was still in the system. He snuck through the back door and waited till the nurses left a computer unattended. He then logged into his old account and smiled to himself when it went through. Gabe quickly filled in Angie's discharge papers before logging off. He then made his way to her room, where he found her in the bed watching a movie on the television above her bed.

"Angel Gabriel, I mean papa," cried Angie, her face lighting up.

"No, it is just Gabe again; we need to leave," said Gabe.

"Then I can see mama?" asked Angie, her face had more colour in it.

Gabe nodded his head and lifted the small girl into his arms; he threw a blanket over her to keep her fully hidden. Gabe stepped out into the hallway, almost freezing in place at the sight of Ashley talking to the head nurse. Gabe ducked back into the room. She was about to look down the hallway, and he would have been seen.

"What is it?" asked Angie, lifting her small head up and peeping out the blanket.

"Nothing, sweetie," whispered Gabe, covering her head with the blanket once more.

He peered out into the empty hallway and quickly made his way out of the building with the little girl in his arms. He waved to the security guard, telling Angie to smile and wave before ducking into the shadows.

Gabe took her home to her mother, who cried tears of joy to see her daughter so healthy.

"Señor Gabe, tell me what I can do to thank you," sobbed Maria, cradling Angie in her arms.

"I want one thing from you, Maria," said Gabe, handing her the envelope filled with money.

Her eyes widened in shock and fear, as she pushed it back towards him.

"No! I cannot take this.," sobbed Maria.

"Yes, you can, and I want you to go to a shelter and tell them that you need help, take this and make a better life for your family."

"They will send me away and my children back."

"No, they won't, Manny and Angie are citizens of this country, and as for you, you can get a study visa and make a better life for yourself," whispered Gabe.

"Thank you, Angel Gabriel, for saving us." Maria wrapped her free arm around him; he stood there awkwardly as he waited for her to pull away.

"I want them both in school and no more of this night work," whispered Gabe.

She nodded her head and put Angie down, going into the small house to pack. Gabe held out his hand for Manny to shake.

"Take care of your mother and sister and work hard in school," said Gabe.

Manny shook his hand, pulling his hand free and wrapping his arms around Gabe's waist.

"Thank you."

Ashley walked towards her front door, when the consistent knocking carried on. She was annoyed that anyone would be here at six in the morning. She flung the door open, ready to give someone a piece of her mind, only to find her older brother Chad standing there. He had a large duffel bag on one shoulder and an apologetic look on his face.

"Chad, what are you doing here?" asked Ashley.

"I am sorry I pushed you to come home," said Chad, wrapping his arms around her.

She hugged her brother back, loving how safe she always felt in his arms.

"You didn't know."

"And that was a big mistake on your part, missy. Now I know you have to work, so I will make myself at home while you go do your thing, and we can talk later," said Chad, kissing her on the forehead.

Ashley pulled on her jacket and left her brother in her apartment. The day went by quite slowly. Ashley was waiting for her shift to finally end so that she could spend some time with her brother. She had just finished handing over their last patient when she caught Karla staring at her computer screen with a look of total confusion on her face. Ashley approached slowly.

"What are you doing!" shouted Ashley, laughing at Karla's startled expression.

Karla scowled at her then went back to her computer.

"What's making you pull that face? It's like you have seen a ghost," said Ashley, leaning across the counter top to see what had her so enthralled.

"I have seen one, well, at least it must be one.," replied Karla, shaking her head.

"What do you mean?"

"We had this little girl here with an infection in her colon, and she was discharged last night."

"And what is the problem with that?"

"The doctor who discharged her has supposedly been dead for three years," answered Karla.

"Huh, that is strange. What is his name?"

"Dr. Gabriel Bennett."

A warning bell went off in Ashley's head. It could be just a random coincidence that she also knew a Gabe. There was no way that the Gabe she knew was a doctor. But then thinking about that tube in the boy's chest had been the job of a professional.

"Let me see his picture." Karla turned the screen slightly towards Ashley.

She looked at the photo and sucked in a breath.

"What is it? Did you know him?"

"No, he just looks like someone I know." "Oh, well, I see your ride is waiting to go," pointed Karla.

Ashley peered over her shoulder, at Romeo calling her over. She rolled her eyes and walked out of the hospital after promising to go for coffee with Karla sometime. Ashley thought about the doctor who was supposedly dead. Why would he want people to think he was dead? She stared out of the window, watching the passing scenery go by.

A flash of brown caught her eye. Ashley sat up and looked back out of the window.

"Stop!" shouted Ashley.

Romeo braked suddenly, causing them both to fly forward from the impact.

"What is wrong?" asked Romeo.

"I just saw something and need to go check it out," replied Ashley, hopping out of the car.

"What must I do?" cried Romeo.

"Go get an ice-cream or something," shouted Ashley, running after her retreating doctor.

"Gabe!" called Ashley.

He stopped walking and turned to face her. She noticed that he looked more exhausted than usual. He crossed his arms over his chest and waited for her to say something.

"I know who you are." He arched a brow, refusing to say anything.

Ashley rolled her eyes and stepped closer.

"What I don't get is why you want people to think you are dead or what you did with that little girl last night," said Ashley.

She watched him go suddenly pale, his expression still blank.

"I don't know what you are talking about," stated Gabe.

"So you aren't the infamous Dr. Gabriel Bennett?" She watched his eyes darken with an unreadable expression before he turned to walk away.

"No, I am not him. You are mistaken," said Gabe.

"Why did you take that girl? Is she alright?" "Ask this Gabriel Bennett you speak so highly of," stated Gabe.

"Why would you want to live on the street when you could be saving lives?" asked Ashley, grabbing onto his arm.

"Because I killed him. Gabriel Bennett had to die, and Gabe, the homeless guy, was born," yelled Gabe, walking away from her.

CHAPTER 6

Gabe sat on top of a rusted pile of junk in the junkyard. Whenever he needed to think, he came here. The junkyard was like a second home to him. Tonight, he had a lot on his mind. Ashley knew who he was, and soon she would know his deepest secret. He knew using his name at a place where she worked was risky, but he had needed to get Angie out of there. He wasn't proud of what he had done, but then he hadn't been proud of anything he had done since making that promise three years ago. He had had a few patients die on his table before; being the best didn't come without a few failures here and there. But choosing to take someone's life willingly was the opposite of what being a doctor meant. How was he supposed to say no when his best friend had asked him to kill him, to not let him suffer? A simple promise of a dying friend, had destroyed everything he had ever worked for. It wasn't the fear of getting caught, because he would have lost his license for that. It was the fact that he had to live with killing his best friend, taking away a husband and father, that had made him leave everything he loved behind.

He was so tired of this life, of living with guilt and unhappiness of taking a life that should never have ended. When his wife Annabel blamed him for killing her husband, she had been right. He had killed him; he had his best friend's blood on his hands. No matter how many times he washed, the blood was always there. Gabe stood up with a sigh. He slowly made his way down the pile of junk and back to the only place that accepted him.

Ashley trudged up the staircase towards her apartment. She had so many questions for Gabe. She wanted to know why he would live on the streets, and why he took that little girl from the hospital. She knew without a doubt that whatever he had done with her had been to help her. No matter what else she thought, he was a good guy. She put her key in the lock, but the door opened before she could turn the handle. She had completely forgotten her brother was here.

"Chad," said Ashley, kicking off her shoes.

"I made us some supper, so go sit down, and I will serve us," replied Chad.

Ashley was in no mood to argue with him, just walking towards the chair and collapsing in it. Her brother walked over with a bowl of chicken noodles, handing her a bowl before sitting down next to her. They ate in silence, the television on a random movie. Neither of them was paying much attention to the movie, both caught up in their own thoughts. Ashley put down her empty bowl and patted her full stomach with a sigh. "

I forgot how good a homemade meal tastes," sighed Ashley.

"You need to cook more," mumbled Chad, through a bite of food.

Ashley stuck out her tongue in a childish manner and stood up.

"I want to go take a shower, and then we can talk," said Ashley, leaving the room.

After her shower, she slipped on comfy clothing and walked back into the sitting room. Her brother stood by the window, staring out at the city below.

"I miss the city sometimes," said Chad.

"I miss the old country life, waking up to the sound of horses," laughed Ashley, sitting down with her feet tucked under her bum.

"You always were the first one up," whispered Chad.

He turned to face her, raw honesty on his face.

"I messed everything up; I tried everything to get you to come home," Chad stated with a hysterical laugh.

"But why would you want to live in a house, where your own father wouldn't protect you?"

"You can't blame yourself, Chad; you just wanted us all to be a family again."

"I know, but I never stopped to ask you why you hated Dad so much or why you left home with barely any money," cried Chad, running a hand through his hair.

"I wouldn't have told you anyway; I just needed a clean break."

"But you didn't just lose your fiancé; you lost everything, and we weren't there to support you."

"And look at me now, I have a place to live and a great job and friends."

"When was the last time you spoke to Mom?" asked Chad.

"Two months ago, she was thinking of coming to visit when Dad felt healthier. I guess that won't happen now."

"I still want you to come home, Ash; I won't guilt you into it or anything. There is a great paramedic position open that side and everything."

"I don't know if I can; give me time to think about it."

"That's fine, I understand, but please just think about saying good bye to Dad."

"Fine, I will think about it; now are you going to tell me why you are really here?" asked Ashley.

Chad rubbed at the back of his neck nervously. He approached Ashley and sat down on the coffee table facing her.

"Since the last time I came to visit, I haven't stopped thinking about Karla," mumbled Chad.

"What? My friend Karla," laughed Ashley.

"Yes, your friend Karla, I was hoping to see her again while I was here."

"You came here for a girl!"

"Not any girl, alright; Karla is different from the girls back home," stated Chad.

"Alright, I get it; don't need to get your panties in a twist. I could perhaps need to call you tomorrow to drop something off while I am eating lunch with Karla," said Ashley.

His face lit up as he pulled her forward and wrapped his arms around her.

"You are the best sister."

"I am your only sister,"

Chad laughed loudly before getting up and sitting down next to her. He had this mischievous look in his eyes.

"No, Chad! Whatever you are thinking, no!" started Ashley, standing up.

"I am just thinking about the last time you got tickled."

"No ways! Never again," cried Ashley, getting up and running out of the room. Her brother's footsteps and laughter followed after her.

Gabe sat against a concrete pillar, eating a sandwich and watching the fire flicker through the holes in the drum. He felt lazy and content sitting here. In the distance, children of all different ages, played a game of tag, while a few of the younger men played with a soccer ball. He dusted his hands and stood up as he decided to join in the game. Gabe loved how care free these people acted; they had nothing yet they acted like they had everything. He was in awe of how some of them survived worse than this and saddened by others who had degrees like himself but weren't able to find a job. The ball rolled towards him; he stuck out his foot and stopped it.

"Are you going to play, Gabriel?" asked the young man.

Gabe nodded his head and kicked the ball back to the person standing closest to him. He took off his brown jacket and threw it down on the dusty floor, rolling up his sleeves and running after the ball. Gabe scored at least two goals; it was early morning, and he was sweating from all the running he had been doing. The ball rolled towards the road; Gabe took off after it and stopped. Ashley stood with the ball under her arm, slowly approaching him. His first instinct was to turn around and leave.

He saw the way she slowly approached him. She was waiting to see if he would reject her. Gabe shook the sweat from his hair and jogged the rest of the way towards her.

"Hi," said Ashley with a shy wave. "Hi," replied Gabe sheepishly.

They hadn't parted on good terms last time, and he kind of felt guilty for the way he had shouted at her. She had just wanted answers, and he had shut her down. Gabe took the ball from her and threw it over his shoulder.

"I am out, guys," shouted Gabe.

"Sorry for last week; I was just shocked to find out who you were. But we all have our secrets; well, you know mine, and you have the right to keep yours."

"I shouldn't have shouted at you; it was a shock to me that you of all people found out who I really was," answered Gabe.

"I know you didn't hurt that girl, so what really happened?"

Gabe sighed and walked towards his jacket, folding it over his arm and motioning for her to follow him.

"Her name is Angie, and she is five years old. I have known her for two years now.," Gabe pointed to the small shelter they had stayed in.

"Their 25-year-old mother came to this country when she was barely a teen and had Manny; he is nine-years-old, and then came Angie. She did what most women did to survive, leaving her son to care for his little sister. I helped out when I could, but it wasn't ideal." "So why didn't you call social services?" asked Ashley.

Gabe gave her a pointed stare; he leaned back against a pillar, crossing his arms.

"They didn't have the ideal life, but they had each other. Maria loves her children, and they love her. Sometimes things aren't always black and white. Angie got a colon infection, and I had taken some morphine for her, hoping to dull the pain. It got worse, and I knew taking her to the hospital would mean taking her from her mother."

"So you pretended to be their father?" asked Ashley, all the pieces coming together.

He gave her a strange look; she moved her hair out of her face.

"Yes, Karla told me about the single father and his sob story and how she was going to call social services but felt bad about it."

"I couldn't let that happen, so I used my password, and I signed her out and brought her back home." "

Where is she now?" asked Ashley.

Gabe pushed off from the pillar, walking in the opposite direction; Ashley ran after him.

"Wait! Where are you going?"

"I want to show you ."

"Something," replied Gabe.

Ashley rolled her eyes as she followed his retreating form. He led them down a few streets, finally stopping in front of a hole-in-the-wall coffee shop.

"Have you got a craving for coffee?" asked Ashley.

"No, look right there," chuckled Gabe, pointing through the window.

Ashley followed his finger, staring past all the customers to a young woman standing behind the counter laughing at something the two small children across from her said.

"That is Maria. I helped her daughter and showed her that there was a better way to make a living or she would lose them,"

Ashley turned to face him, shocked that a guy would do that for someone.

"You did that?"

"No, she did it. I just told her what would happen if she didn't."

The door opened next to them, the bell jingled just before two small bodies flew past her and into Gabe's arms.

"Angel Gabriel, you came to visit," cried Angie.

"I said I would. Have you been good for your mother?" asked Gabe, propping the girl on his hip.

"Si, we have a bed to sleep in and I go to school to learn to be a doctor like you," answered Manny.

Gabe laughed and ruffled the boy's hair affectionately, then turned to face Ashley.

"Manny, Angie, this is my good friend Ashley. She was the one that gave me the medicine for Angie," introduced Gabe.

Manny smiled and ran towards her, wrapping his arms around her waist.

"Thank you for helping us.," whispered Manny.

Ashley fought back emotions, trying not to cry in front of these strangers. She patted Manny on the back and met Gabe's concerned gaze. Ashley gave him a reassuring smile and swiped at the tears running down her cheeks. The door opened again, and Maria stuck her head out.

"Manny, Angie, your food is getting cold," called Maria.

"Coming, mama," called the children.

Gabe put Angie down and said good bye as they watched the children go back inside.

"I know what you did was wrong, but I also know why you did it, and I would have probably done the same thing."

"I didn't tell you so that you would think I was a good guy. I am not a good guy."

"So far, everything shows me differently, but if you want to keep thinking that, then go ahead," smiled Ashley.

"Our worlds are very different, Ashley," said Gabe. "No, they aren't. Just because you live on the street doesn't make you less human than anyone else."

Together, they walked back to the bridge, both lost in their own thoughts.

Gabe stopped near a barrel with a half-dead fire in it, waiting for Ashley to join him. Together, they stood with their fingers over the cooling heat.

"I have a sister. She doesn't live far from here," said Gabe.

"Does she know that you are living like this?" Gabe gave a sad laugh, his eyes showing emotions he tried best to keep hidden.

"Her older brother lives on the street. Why would I want her to know that?"

"Because she loves you."

"Not after what I did."

"What did you do?" asked Ashley, shivering slightly at the haunted look in his eyes.

Gabe opened and closed his mouth a few times, staring past her, lost in his own memories. He turned and looked her straight in the eye, regret for what he was about to say already eminent.

"I killed my best friend," answered Gabe, withdrawing physically and emotionally.

Ashley's mind came up with a thousand different things he could mean by the one statement. Her mind reeling from all the recent knowledge she had just gained. She opened her mouth to say something when suddenly they heard the sound of a body hitting cement and a gut-wrenching scream.

They both turned around to see a body lying on the ground in the road; the person had jumped from the bridge. Gabe and Ashley took off in a run towards the body. Ashley pulled out her cell phone and called for an ambulance. They both knelt on either side of the young woman's body. Gabe looked up at Ashley, and she nodded her head. Slowly, they rolled the body, nausea rolling through them at the sight of her mangled face. It wouldn't come as a surprise if she had broken every bone in her body. Gabe checked for a pulse while she directed the ambulance to their location.

"She has a faint pulse," said Gabe.

"How is she even alive still?" cried Ashley, staring up at the bridge.

"That is at least 200 feet or more."

"We need to stop some of the bleeding," said Ashley.

"She is practically dead, and if she does survive, then she will live her life as a vegetable," answered Gabe.

Ashley glared at Gabe. He sighed and lifted her pants leg. The bone stuck out of the skin, blood pouring from the wound.

"There is nothing that can be done here. She needs medical help we can't give."

"But you are a doctor, and I am a paramedic. There must be something that can be done?" cried Ashley.

The next moment, a small boy came running towards them, screaming and crying. Gabe stood up and ran towards the boy, grabbing him up into his arms, hiding him from the scene behind him.

In the distance, they heard ambulance sirens approaching. The boy looked to be about six years old, tears running down his cheeks as he fought Gabe.

"That's my mommy," screamed the boy.

Gabe's heart broke for the little boy whose mother had dared to jump while her son was around.

"My friend is trying to help your mommy, and help is on the way, but you can't see her yet," said Gabe.

The boy burst into another fresh bout of tears, rubbing his nose onto Gabe's dirty shirt.

"She said she could fly," the boy said with hiccupping sobs.

Gabe kept the boy hidden from the scene behind them. He sat down behind the pillar with the boy in his lap.

"What is your name?" asked Gabe, rubbing a soothing hand down the boy's back.

"Travis. My daddy is at work, and he is going to be upset that mommy is hurt," whispered the boy.

"I will tell my friend to call him right away. Why don't you tell me what happened?"

"Mommy was feeling tired this morning. She shouted at me and said I was being too loud. She told me to get in the car and that we were going to go for a trip," sobbed the boy.

"And then what happened?"

"I was singing my songs in the car, and she stopped the car. She screamed at me and told me to wait in the car while she went to fly like Peter Pan."

"You know people can't really fly?" replied Gabe, his anger boiling for what this poor boy had been through.

"I saw her climb on the rail. She looked at me and waved. Then she was gone, and she never came back. I want my mommy. Please take me to her," cried Travis.

"I can't do that, Travis. I need you to be brave for me. Can you do that?" asked Gabe, his voice rising with his emotions.

Ashley peered around the corner, taking in the scene ahead of her of the two of them sitting there. She slowly approached them, crouching down in front of Travis.

"Hi, I am Ashley, Gabe's friend, and I was thinking that maybe you would like to take a ride with me to go see your daddy?" said Ashley.

The boy lifted up his head, his face flushed from crying.

"And mommy?" squeaked Travis.

"She is already in the ambulance on her way."

Travis nodded his head and flung himself forward into Ashley's arms. Gabe placed a hand on her knee, asking the silent question. Ashley shook her head, tears filling her eyes as she stood up with Travis in her arms. Gabe sat there long after they had left, staring down at the blood drying on his hands.

CHAPTER 7

Ashley sat in bed, her legs crossed, and her laptop on her lap. She was online and searching for anything related to Doctor Gabriel Bennett. His last comment to her had really stuck with her. What did he mean when he said he had killed someone? She typed in his name and pressed search. A dozen articles came up, all about the handsome young doctor who was making his way up in the medical world. Some of the articles mentioned that he was one of the best neurosurgeons in the country. However, the last few articles about Gabriel were about his best friend dying after an operation performed by Doctor Bennett, and the same day Gabriel Bennett boarded his private yacht never to be seen again. Some say he fell overboard, others say he jumped off the boat, or just ran away. There were very few articles about his family; other than his sister, there was no one else. She wondered why a man who had everything would walk away from it all because of a patient's death. In their world, deaths were pretty common, so what made this one so different? Besides, it was his closest friend. Ashley yawned loudly in her silent apartment, and after reading one more article, she shut down her laptop.

She knew she was thinking too much about Gabe, but he never strayed far from her thoughts. Just when she thought she had him figured out, he threw her a curve ball. She could still see him sitting on the dirty floor under the bridge with the small boy Travis crying in his arms. He had just held the little boy while they took his mother away. Ashley sighed in frustration and curled up in bed. She would figure him out; it couldn't be that hard, she thought.

The next morning, she got ready for work earlier than usual, taking the long way around to work, so that she could pass by the bridge. It was mostly empty at this time of morning; the sun had been up for a while now. She sighed and drove off to work. She was practically stalking the guy. If he had Facebook, she would probably be his biggest stalker. She needed to go on a date to get her mind off Gabe. Later that day, after getting their patient settled, Ashley went in search of Romeo and found him flirting with the nursing staff. She rolled her eyes and leaned across the counter next to him, their shoulders touching.

"Hey girls, did Romeo here tell you the time that he wet his... mhmhmhmm," mumbled Ashley behind the hand Romeo had placed over her mouth.

"Ladies, if you will excuse us," said Romeo with a flash of his dimple.

He still had his hand over Ashley's mouth, leading her outside to the loading dock.

"What were you doing back there?" asked Romeo, taking his hand away and crossing his arms over his chest.

"Relax, Romeo, I wasn't going to tell them anything," giggled Ashley.

Romeo eyed her suspiciously.

"And what has, or should I say who has, put you in such a good mood? I haven't seen you like this for a while," replied Romeo.

"Oh, nothing much, just that I have a date with Dr. Denver of pediatrics," said Ashley with a slight squeal.

"Seriously? I heard all the nurses have been trying for months to get him to ask them out; he turns each of them down."

"And I bet you give them your shoulder to cry on," teased Ashley.

"Well, I can't let them cry alone in the bathroom," winked Romeo, and with one last chuckle, he led them to the ambulance.

Ashley was slightly nervous; she hadn't been on a date in a year or two. When Dr. Zack Denver had walked up to her and asked her out this morning, her first thought was to tell him no. But then she thought of Gabe and quickly said yes; maybe a night out with Zack would help her get over Gabe.

Gabe sat on an overturned crate, watching the empty spot where she had killed herself, now filled with flowers. He still didn't know what made a woman jump like that, especially with her child in the car. Someone had placed a cross with a photo of her family attached to it. The rest of the day, people gathered in groups, placing flowers and teddy bears around the cross. He watched as the day drew on, the crowds grew, and so did the flowers. This woman had been loved by many, and she had decided to forgo it all, for what? A few lit candles were placed here and there. Gabe stood up, stretching his arm muscles and rolling his neck side to side. He walked slowly around the memorial, wondering if it was worth it for her to be remembered this way. "Gabe!" shouted a small voice. Gabe turned around to face an older man holding the little boy Travis in his arms. Travis had a colourful bouquet of daisies in one hand and a card in the other.

"Hey, Travis, I see you brought flowers," said Gabe.

"These were my mommy's favourite," replied Travis sadly.

"Travis, why don't you go put that down while I talk to Gabe here," said the father as he put his son down.

Gabe waited for the man to speak first.

"I heard that you stopped my son from seeing his mother like that," started the man.

Gabe opened his mouth but was stopped by the man holding up a hand.

"Please don't, I will always be grateful that his last memory of her wasn't seeing her mangled body."

"I am sorry for your loss."

"I have been hearing that all day, and it makes me want to laugh. People who die in accidents or from sickness, loved ones need to hear that. But when your wife takes your son with her and makes him watch her jump, then there isn't much loss to be had, is there!" sighed the man dejectedly.

"I am sure she loved you and Travis very much. I can't tell you why she did it, and maybe you will never know. But be grateful she didn't take Travis with her," said Gabe.

The man's body trembled slightly at that thought.

"I guess I have one thing to thank her for then. Now I have to go home and explain to my son that him shouting and making a noise didn't make his mother kill herself."

Gabe clapped the man on the shoulder and waved goodbye to Travis. Travis tugged on his father's hand, making him stop walking. He turned and looked over his shoulder at Gabe.

"Mister Gabe, you will watch after my mommy's flowers, won't you?" called Travis.

"Yeah, buddy, of course I will," answered Gabe.

He saw the look of gratitude in the father's eyes and turned back to face the collection of flowers. Gabe stood there for a while, the urge to see Ashley growing by the minute.

Ashley looked at her reflection in the mirror once more. She reapplied the red lipstick to her lips and smiled. Tonight she would go out and forget all about Gabe; tonight was about having fun. She picked up her small black clutch purse that matched her strapless black knee-length dress and red stilettos. Her stomach fluttered nervously at the thought of going on a date. Zack was everything Gabe wasn't; even his looks were far from Gabe's. Where Gabe had long black hair, Zack had short blonde hair. Gabe had blue eyes, and Zack had grey eyes. So tonight there would be no comparing them or anything; the two men were totally opposite from each other. Her buzzer went off, and with one last look in the mirror, Ashley grabbed her jersey and walked out of the door. Zack stood outside wearing black dress pants and a white open-collar shirt. He smiled and handed her the bunch of red roses in his hand.

Ashley smiled in return and brought them towards her nose to smell them.

"I thought we could go have a nice quiet dinner and then a moonlight stroll in the park," said Zack, holding out his arm for her.

Ashley slipped her arm in his as she let him lead her to his black sports car. As she slipped into the passenger seat, she looked up and straight at Gabe, who stood leaning against the tree outside the apartment, with his hands in his worn jeans pockets. Ashley sucked in a breath, instantly feeling guilty. Her cheeks flooded with colour at the thought of him seeing her with another man. It wasn't like they had anything going on between them. But seeing the sadness and acceptance in Gabe's eyes burnt right to her soul. She looked down at the red roses lying across her lap, waiting for Zack to start the car.

"Where are we eating?" asked Ashley.

"I got us a reservation at Zoe's Kitchen," replied Zack, pulling away.

Ashley looked up into the rear view mirror, her eyes catching Gabe's startling blue eyes. She averted her eyes with a sigh.

"Are you alright? You don't seem yourself," questioned Zack.

"Sorry, I have a lot on my mind with work and family."

"Let's not think about that; let's just enjoy our time together tonight," smiled Zack, placing his hand on top of hers on her thigh.

Dinner was actually interesting; Zack was smart and funny, and he listened to everything she had to say. They spent almost three hours in the restaurant eating and talking, and afterwards Zack led her through the park along the brightly lit path around the pond.

Ashley stared out at the rippling water around them, watching the ducks dipping under the water. She shivered slightly, and Zack slipped his black coat off and gently placed it over her shoulders. She smiled and took his hand in hers. It had been a long time since she had enjoyed an evening in a man's company. But there was no spark with Zack; he just felt safe, and that was what she had always wanted until Gabe entered the picture.Everything was always about Gabe; why was he always in her thoughts?

"Zack, you have been at the hospital for years now, right?"

"Yeah, almost seven years. Why?"

"Do you remember a doctor called Gabriel Bennett?" asked Ashley nervously.

They stopped walking, and he turned to look at her, a sad look in his eyes.

"Yes, we were pretty close back in the day. He was a great doctor and he saved so many lives, but sometimes there is that one patient that gets to you, and it destroys you when you can't save them."

"Is that what happened to Gabe?"

"The patient was his friend, and that makes it worse. I wish I knew what happened to him," he gave her a puzzled look.

"Wait, why did you call him Gabe?"

"I just naturally shortened his name, I guess," lied Ashley.

He got this thoughtful look in his eyes before lifting his hand and gently moving a strand of hair out of her face.

"I had fun tonight, Ashley. I would love to see you again," whispered Zack.

They heard a noise behind them and turned around. Ashley saw the familiar brown coat and froze. She watched Gabe dig through the dustbin next to the park bench. She looked up at Zack, who had a look of sorrow on his face.

"Come on, let's go. I feel sorry for these guys that have to scratch for other people's food," said Zack.

"They have to survive somehow," answered Ashley, knowing Gabe could hear everything they were saying.

"Still, this is a public place," stated Zack, letting go of Ashley's hand and turning to face Gabe.

"Hey, you digging in the bin over there, here is some leftovers," shouted Zack.

Ashley wanted to curl into a ball and die from humiliation; she watched Gabe turn and look straight at her before taking the bag from Zack and turning to go. Her blood boiled, her temper flaring, at the fact that he would do something like that. Gabe had done it on purpose. He had wanted her to see the difference between Zack and himself. She crossed her arms, silently fuming inside and followed Zack back to the car.

The next day, Ashley was in a bad mood; the whole night she had thought about what Gabe had done. Romeo kept a wide berth between them as she glared at him.

"I guess the date didn't go well?"

"No, it actually went great." "And you are in a bad mood why then?" chuckled Romeo.

"I just am, Romeo!" growled Ashley.

He rolled his eyes and climbed into the ambulance.

"Woman!" grumbled Romeo.

Ashley hid a grin behind a fake cough and waited for Romeo to start the car. They had just received a call that an old man was having a heart attack and needed assistance right away. They put the sirens on and followed the directions. Ashley grabbed her medical bag and followed Romeo towards the house. They knocked on the door with no reply.

"We are coming in to see if you need help," shouted Romeo through the closed door.

He turned the handle, and the door opened. They entered the house and found an older man lying on his kitchen floor with the phone lying sideways and the dialling tone playing. Ashley knelt down next to the man, checking his pulse.

"He has a pulse, but it is weak," said Ashley.

Romeo took out the neck brace and helped her place it around his neck.

"Sir, can you hear us? We are here to help you," called Ashley.

"He is non-responsive," said Romeo into his radio attached to his waist.

They quickly and efficiently placed him onto the gurney and attached an I.V bag before checking his heart rate again. They hurried back out the door towards the ambulance. Ashley groaned in frustration at the sight of the open doors. Romeo rolled his eyes and helped her slide the gurney in the back. Ashley got in and shut the doors.

"Was it our mystery thief?" asked Romeo.

"Yes."

.

The minute her shift ended, Ashley drove straight towards the bridge. She parked her car and walked towards the bridge. She stopped a few feet away, staring at the sight of Gabe bending down and removing dead daisies from the memorial and replacing them with new ones.

"What are you doing?" asked Ashley, placing her hands on her hips.

Gabe jumped slightly, before carrying on with his job. When he was done, he stood up with ease and turned to face her.

"Keeping a promise," replied Gabe.

"You are big on keeping promises, I see," stated Ashley.

She saw a glimpse of pain and guilt flash through his eyes, before he masked it with indifference. She wanted to probe, but she had come here for a reason.

"What are you doing here, Ashley?" asked Gabe wearily.

"I know why you did what you did last night."

"I don't know what you are talking about," replied Gabe with an air of arrogance.

Ashley's temper flared at his remark; she stormed towards him and pushed him backward.

"Don't lie to me; you saw me with your friend Zack and decided to show me the difference in our worlds," shouted Ashley.

"Zack is a great guy," whispered Gabe.

"Zack is a nice guy, but he isn't you," yelled Ashley, pushing him again.

"Stop pushing me," growled Gabe, grabbing onto her wrist.

"Then stop pushing me away."

"You are the one that went on a date, Ashley. What game do you think this is? This is my life, and I live here. Right here where you are standing, you deserve better than that."

"Why don't you deserve better?" asked Ashley, lifting her free hand to touch his clean-shaven cheek.

She saw pain flash in his beautiful blue eyes and stepped closer.

"Don't," pleaded Gabe, pulling his face away.

Nothing you say will make me go away," replied Ashley, pulling her hand free from his grip and placing them both flat onto his chest.

She watched him swallow nervously. He looked ready to run any minute.

"I killed a patient and a friend. You don't understand, Ashley, that I deserve this. Living here is where I belong after what I did," answered Gabe with an air of defeat.

He closed his eyes, trying to block out the sight of her probing green eyes.

"Everyone accidentally kills a patient; it doesn't mean they deserve to die to the world they live in," answered Ashley, running her hand up and down his chest.

He sucked in a deep breath; she looked up at him, and he nearly stepped back at the look in his eyes. He let out a soft groan, before his head descended, and his lips gently touched hers. Ashley gasped and slipped her hands up and into his thick hair. He wrapped his arms around her waist and lifted her slightly, bringing their bodies flush against each other. She moaned into the kiss as her lips parted slightly, giving him entry. They stood for a while under a dirty bridge, kissing and hands roaming as things grew heated between them. Finally, Gabe pulled up for air, his eyes hazy. Hers looked no better. Ashley hadn't realised that he had lifted her slightly off the ground, her feet touching the ground as he slowly let her go. She pulled her hands out of his hair and ran it down his arms. Biting her lips, she gave him a shy smile before gently leaning her forehead against his chest and laughing. She wondered what he thought of her; she was acting like a crazy woman. But he just stood there and let her laugh.

"Stop stealing my medicine," said Ashley between bursts of giggles.

Gabe looked up at the blue sky above and laughed; his whole chest vibrated with each chuckle. Once they had both calmed down, Gabe suddenly sobered up and stood looking at her with sadness in his eyes.

"Zack is still a nice guy," whispered Gabe.

Ashley glared at him and swatted him on the chest playfully; he pouted and rubbed at his chest.

"You are a better kisser," teased Ashley.

She saw the look of jealousy in his eyes and hid her grin.

He grabbed her hand in his larger one and pulled her further under the bridge.

"Where are you taking me?" asked Ashley.

"I want to show you something," said Gabe.

Gabe felt lighter than he had in years, after kissing Ashley. He pulled her past people standing in groups and out the other side of the bridge.

"Where are you taking me?" asked Ashley.

"To your medicine," answered Gabe.

Ashley stared at the back of his head, confused but intrigued at the same time. She let him lead her through the streets until they arrived at a run-down building, that looked ready to be condemned. Gabe still held tightly onto her hand, showing her a part of his world, hoping she would understand. He led her inside the building, the smell of faeces and other filth assaulting their noses. He was used to the smell but knew it would be horrible for Ashley. He turned back and gave her a sheepish smile, which she returned, giving their joined hand a squeeze. Gabe led her up a small flight of stairs. The ground was covered in unimaginable things, so he tried to take the clearest path available. At the top of the stairs, Gabe walked over to the first door and knocked on it three times. He heard childish screams and laughter on the other side, before the door was pulled open. He braced himself as three small bodies slammed into him. "

Angel Gabriel!" shouted the children.

Gabe smiled and patted each child on the head in greeting.

"Chris, Annie, and Mike, this is my friend Ashley. She wanted to say hi to you guys and to see your mommy," said Gabe.

The oldest of the three, who looked to be seven years old, stepped forward.

"Mama is having a bad day today; she is lying down," replied Chris.

"Who is at the door, Annie?" shouted a frail voice from inside.

"It is Angel Gabriel, and he brought a girl with him," giggled Annie.

Ashley smiled and waved at the youngest child, Mike, who hid his face in Gabe's pants.

Gabe chuckled and bent down to lift the toddler into his arms.

"I came to see how you are doing and to bring a friend of mine; she is the one who gives us all the medicine," called Gabe, entering the house with the children.

"Give!" whispered Ashley.

Gabe smiled and passed her the boy in his arms. Ashley gladly took hold of the little boy, a handsome little guy with chocolate brown eyes and brown curls falling into his eyes. He smiled and popped his dirty thumb into his mouth. Gabe walked into the small sitting room and looked over at the frail young woman lying down. Her skin was paler than usual, with a thin sheen of sweat coating her body.

"On a scale, how bad?" asked Gabe, kneeling down in front of her.

"Seven," whispered the woman, closing her eyes.

"Are you lying to me?" questioned Gabe, checking her pulse.

"Maybe an eight," replied the woman with a weak smile.

Gabe nodded his head and took out a small bottle of pills, handing her two. She sat up with his help and took them with a glass of water.

"You need to get to a doctor," said Gabe.

"Lenny works so hard to give us food and clothing. We just can't waste the money."

"I know it is hard, Janet, but what happens to these three if something happens to you?"

"Nothing will happen to me; it is just a bad day today."

"Alright, I will be by next week to check on you again. Kids, be good and take care of your mother," said Gabe, handing them each a sucker.

Ashley placed the boy in her arms down and followed Gabe out of the small flat.

"What is wrong with her?" asked Ashley.

"She has chronic back pain all the time," said Gabe.

"But she is so young!"

"And she was lifting heavy objects for a living."

"Is everyone here as bad as her?" asked Ashley, rubbing her arms.

"Yes," answered Gabe, leading her to the next door.

An hour later, they exited the building, breathing in clean, fresh air. Gabe turned to face Ashley, his eyes filled with emotions.

"I know taking the medicine is wrong and that you can get into trouble for it, but it helps them," said Gabe.

"I know why you do it, but it is still wrong, Gabe. Besides, if you were still a doctor, think about what you could do with the money you made. You could save lives."

"It isn't that simple!"

"Then explain it to me," pleaded Ashley.

"I can't; you just have to trust me on that. I have one more place I want to show you."

Ashley nodded her head and let Gabe lead her away from all the pain and suffering they had just seen.

Gabe led her towards the junkyard; he had never brought anyone here before. He led her through the gap in the fence and around piles of junk. Gabe helped her to climb to the top, where they sat on a broken chair.

"So this is your favourite place?" said Ashley. "Yes."

"Why?" questioned Ashley, looking around the piles of junk.

"Just wait for it," whispered Gabe into her ear.

He faced forward, hearing her gasp from beside him. He turned to look at her, seeing awe written all over her face. He looked forward at the sun descending, reflecting through different pieces of junk. It was truly a spectacular view. He turned back to find her staring at him.

"I thought my spot was good," whispered Ashley.

"It reminds me to look for the good in everything, even in the worst of places," answered Gabe.

She looked at him, like he was someone more than a homeless guy. She made him feel alive inside, and he knew she deserved better, but he was selfish enough to want her for himself. Gabe placed his finger under her chin and tilted her face upwards. He loved to see the surprise flicker in her green eyes just before his lips descended onto hers. He kept the kiss light and gentle, as they sat on a pile of junk, the sun setting in front of them.

CHAPTER 8

Gabe stood partly hidden behind a large oak tree, with a ball cap on his head. It was a risky move to be out here, so close to his sister, but today was an important day for them both. He watched his sister bend down in front of the two gravestones, her long black hair like a curtain around her face. He longed to walk over to her and pull her into his arms as they cried together over the loss of their parents. But she had her husband Luke and her beautiful daughter Gabriella to comfort her; he wasn't needed. His eyes stung with tears as he watched his baby sister's shoulders shake with sobs. Gabriella walked over to her mother and gently grabbed her mother's cheeks between her small hands.

"Mommy, don't be sad," cried the toddler.

"Gabby, leave mommy; she is saying goodbye to her mommy and daddy," replied Luke, holding out his hand for her to take.

Andy turned and pulled her daughter into her arms, the little girl bending forward and rubbing their noses together affectionately.

"I love you, mommy."

"I love you, baby," whispered Andy.

Gabe wiped his eyes on the back of his hand, knowing moments like these would never happen for him. He watched Luke kneel down next to her and wrap his arms around them both.

"I wish Gabe was here with us," whispered Andy.

"I think we need to move on with our life, Andy."

"He is my brother, Luke. I know he just left, but he had his reasons, and I just want him to come home," cried Andy.

"I know, baby. I would love for my friend to come home and see his niece. But Gabe will do what he needs to do, and maybe I think he is being selfish in letting us believe he is dead, but he has his reasons," replied Luke with a kiss on her head.

"Can we go home now, mommy?" asked Gabby.

Andy nodded her head and stood up; she turned around, and it looked like she was looking straight at him. Gabe ducked behind the tree, his heart beating fast. He waited a second or two before peering out the side. He watched them walk back to their car with their daughter walking between them, holding their hands.

He waited for their car to completely disappear before stepping out from behind the tree and walking towards the two people that had meant the world to him. He knelt down in front of the two small, but elegant headstones and placed a single white daisy in front of his mother's stone. Gabe stared at the two names carved in stone, 'Nicholas and Sophia Bennett,' and felt tears run down his cheeks.

"I am sorry for being a disappointment, mama. I failed you and papa," whispered Gabe.

He placed his hand onto the flat surface of his father's stone.

"You taught me to be a better man, and I didn't listen. I broke my promise to care for Andy, and I ran away. She deserves better than to have me as a brother," sobbed Gabe, his large shoulders shaking.

"I miss you two every day. I miss mama scolding me for not giving her grandchildren and for the times we shared a beer out back, dad. I wanted to make you two proud, but instead, I became this."

He sat alone in the graveyard, his chest heaving as great big sobs escaped. He sat crying for the life he had lost and the woman that he was falling for but would never be good enough for.

He wanted to have a house and a family. He wanted those things with Ashley.

"I found a woman you would have loved, but I am not the man she needs. She makes me want to do better for myself and others."

He sat there for a half-hour just talking to the headstones about everything that had happened in his life. He had lost his parents five years ago in a fatal car accident, yet it sometimes seemed like it was only yesterday.

Ashley finished her early morning jog, her heart beating fast and her body covered in sweat. She turned the music off on her iPod and climbed into a cool shower. She hadn't heard anything from her brothers, begging her to come home, and that suited her just fine. Today, the hospital was having a charity cook-off in the hospital courtyard, for all the patients and their families. There would be hamburgers and chips, games, and rides. They did this every year, and it seemed to be growing larger each year. Ashley had wanted to invite Gabe but knew that he would not come. She still wanted to know why he had walked away from being a doctor. What he did now was good, but he could do more as a doctor and still help those less fortunate in need. She got out of the shower and slipped into a pair of denim shorts and a loose pink tank top with her gold sandals. Today was about having fun, being alive, and having something to look forward to. She grabbed her jacket and a small backpack before leaving the house. Ashley drove over to the hospital; the place was packed already. There were balloons everywhere and a large colourful jumping castle. The patients and their families were mixing with doctors and nurses, as staff switched shifts. Ashley searched the area until she found Karla standing and talking to someone with his back to her, but he looked familiar.

"Karla!" called Ashley, approaching her friend.

They both turned to face her, and she gasped out loud and smiled excitedly at the sight of her brother Chad. Ashley ran towards him as he pulled her into a hug.

"I didn't know you were coming?" cried Ashley.

"Karla invited me, free food and drinks. How could I say no?" laughed Chad as he let her go.

"I see you have my brother on a tight leash," giggled Ashley, hugging her friend in greeting.

"Your brother is the perfect gentleman," answered Karla.

"Hey Ash, I signed us up for the ball tossing," yelled Romeo, approaching the small group.

Ashley turned to face her friend; he had on black shorts and a navy blue button-down shirt. Life would be so much easier if she fell in love with Romeo.

"Hey Romeo, this is my older brother Chad," said Ashley.

"So you are the young man that has taken my little sis under his wing," stated Chad.

"Well, I wouldn't," stammered Romeo. Ashley smacked her brother on the arm and laughed.

"Ouch," grumbled Chad, rubbing the spot.

"He is pulling your leg."

"Well, I wouldn't say that, but I am grateful that you have kept an eye on her for me," said Chad.

Romeo gave her a look that said she should come clean to her brother. Ashley glared back, and he surrendered at her stern glare. Chad looked between the two of them and hooked an arm around Romeo's neck.

"Why don't we go find something to drink and leave the ladies to chat?" stated Chad, steering Romeo towards the drinks stand.

He stopped and looked over his shoulder straight at Ashley.

"And Ash, we will be talking later!" called Chad before he was enveloped in a crowd of people with Romeo. Ashley groaned and turned to face Karla; her friend had her hands on her hips.

"And what was that about?" asked Karla.

"I found a guy." "

You what? Really? I have to meet him," cried Karla.

"You can't," mumbled Ashley.

"And why not, I won't try to steal him. Your brother is keeping me on my toes as it is," giggled Karla.

Ashley opened her mouth to reply, but was saved from answering as Zack approached them. He looked exhausted and worried; Ashley turned her concerned gaze towards him.

"Why are you looking like someone has just driven over your cat?" asked Ashley.

"It sure feels like it," sighed Zack, rubbing his temples.

"Why don't you tell Nurse Karla all about it?" teased Karla.

He turned to them with a defeated shrug.

"I have a fifteen-year-old patient with a large tumour on his spine," said Zack.

"Oh no! How is he holding up?" cried Ashley.

"Not good actually. I haven't performed a surgery like this before, and there are no other doctors at the hospital that have. It is dangerous, and one slip could paralyze him for life."

"But surely there is someone that can do the surgery?" asked Ashley.

"No, he is right. Dr. Gabriel Bennett was our top neurosurgeon, and he was the only one that was able to do those types of surgeries," answered Karla.

Ashley stood very still, her heart rate picking up at the sound of Gabe's name.

"His parents' insurance only covers this hospital, and no doctor will come perform the surgery here."

Ashley stood there, people passing them by as her mind ran wild. She turned to where Zack was pointing towards a lanky teenage boy sitting in a wheelchair with a small girl on his lap and an eleven-year-old boy pushing his wheelchair.

"And there is nothing else that can be done?" asked Ashley.

"No, I will try to give him treatment and pain meds, but he will have to be discharged, and over time, he will die," sighed Zack.

Ashley bit her lip to stop herself from saying anything that could cause more harm; she listened to the rest of their conversation in silence. Shortly afterwards, Zack excused himself and left for an emergency surgery. Ashley left Karla with her brother and tried to relax and enjoy the rest of the day. But her mind was filled with thoughts of the young boy and of Gabe.

That evening, she walked into her apartment exhausted, her head pounding. She took two aspirins and pulled out her laptop, searching for Gabriel Bennett again and reading over the many surgeries he had done. She knew that she couldn't just sit with this information; Gabe could save this boy's life. She yawned and left her laptop on the open page of Gabe as she fell asleep.

Gabe stretched out his tired muscles and peeped under his shirt at the small black kitten asleep in the crook of his arm. He had found the rest of the litter dead, and this one was the sole survivor. It was dark, and the poor thing shivered slightly before letting out a small cry. He couldn't keep the kitten or leave it here to die. Gabe made up his mind and turned to walk to Ashley's apartment. He hadn't seen her in almost a week, and he was keen on seeing her. He slipped through the dark, stopping in front of the familiar building. Gabe rang the intercom and waited on the front steps, the kitten waking up hungry and crying. After what seemed like forever, but was probably only five minutes later, a groggy voice answered.

"Hello!" mumbled the voice.

"Ashley, it is Gabe. Sorry if I woke you. I could come back tomorrow," said Gabe, standing up.

"No! I was just having a quick power nap. Please come right up," replied Ashley.

Gabe waited for the door to buzz open and entered, with the kitten still in hand. He jogged up the two flights, her door already open for him. Gabe walked inside, his tense muscles relaxing at the sight of Ashley sitting on the couch looking all dishevelled and sleepy.

"Hi, I brought you something," said Gabe, sticking his hand down his shirt and pulling out a small ball of black fluff.

Her eyes lit up, and she jumped up, taking the kitten from him.

"I didn't know if you would want it, but the rest of his brothers and sisters are dead," said Gabe, rubbing the back of his neck nervously.

Ashley cuddled the kitten to her chest and smiled.

"Why don't you take a seat, and I will make us some coffee and this little cutie something to eat," said Ashley, gesturing towards the chairs.

Gabe nodded and took off his jacket, hating that he had to sit with his dirty clothing on her clean furniture. He sat there looking around the room. The last time he had been in so much pain, he had barely noticed his surroundings. He looked down at the coffee table and at the photo frame sitting next to her laptop. Gabe picked up the photo with a fond smile on his face. Ashley looked to be sixteen or so in the picture, her arm around an older guy that could only be her father. They both looked happy and carefree. He had been staring so intently at the picture that he hadn't heard her enter.

"That was still when my father was my hero," said Ashley.

Gabe looked up at her and quickly put the frame back. He accidentally knocked it over onto her laptop. Gabe leaned forward and picked it up. The screen lit up accidentally, and he found himself staring at a photo of him taken four years ago. His eyes widened, and he turned to look at Ashley. She had a guilty-looking expression on her face. She approached him and slammed the screen shut.

"That isn't what it looks like," said Ashley.

"You were looking me up," croaked Gabe, more shaken at seeing his former self than he would admit.

"Yes, I was, but there is a reason for that," stated Ashley, biting her lip nervously.

Gabe stood up and faced her; she stared straight back at him.

"I had to see if you were as good as they said."

"Why? Is how I am not good enough for you?" asked Gabe, crossing his arms defensively.

"No! You are perfect just the way you are, Gabe. But there is this boy, and he is only fifteen, and he needs surgery."

"NO!" stated Gabe with a finality that scared her.

"You didn't let me finish."

"You don't need to. I will not go back there."

"He is fifteen, and he will eventually die if he doesn't get the surgery he needs. Please, Gabe, just think about that," pleaded Ashley, grabbing onto his arm.

"I never asked for any of this, I never asked for you to follow me or anything. I want you to stay out of my life and leave me alone," yelled Gabe, his eyes blazing with anger.

"Just tell me why you won't do this," cried Ashley.

"I don't have to tell you anything," growled Gabe, pulling his arm free from her tight grasp.

"I deserve to know, Gabe, if you care anything about me at all."

"I don't," answered Gabe, his face guarded.

Ashley felt her heart shatter at his words. She wanted to fall to her knees and cry. She looked into the cold face of Gabe, who had suddenly become a stranger to her. A voice startled them out of the tense moment.

"What is going on here?" shouted a male voice from the door.

Gabe turned to face the intruder, seeing an older version of the man she had called her brother a few weeks ago.

"Chad, what are you doing here?" cried Ashley.

"I came to check on you, and I am glad I did. I heard you shouting from downstairs."

"We were just having a disagreement," stated Ashley.

Gabe gave a loud snort and turned to her brother.

"I was just leaving."

"No, Gabe, please don't go. Let's talk this over," begged Ashley. He looked at her with cold, emotionless eyes and pushed past her brother, leaving her alone with no answers.

CHAPTER 9

Gabe stood partly hidden behind a large oak tree, with a ball Ashley ran a hand through her long hair, giving it a frustrated tug. She watched her brother slam the door closed and face her with brotherly concern. Ashley stood her ground, waiting for the lecture that was bound to come.

"I just want to ask you one thing, is your new boyfriend a homeless guy?" asked Chad.

Ashley looked up at her brother and burst into laughter, it came from deep within. She stood there looking like a maniac, tears running down her face as she laughed. Chad looked at her with concerned eyes, and she felt her walls tumbling. Her laughter turned into sobs as she felt her brother wrap his arms around her. Ashley buried her face in his top and cried; he just stood there and let her. After a few minutes, she pulled back and wiped her eyes.

"He was my boyfriend, or kind of, I think," mumbled Ashley.

Chad smiled and touched his finger to the tip of her nose.

"Only you, Ash, only you," laughed Chad.

"He won't ever talk to me again," sobbed Ashley.

Chad rolled his eyes and pulled her towards the chair; he sat down and pulled her down next to him.

"Ash, when did you get a cat?" asked Chad, staring at the black ball of fur that was cautiously approaching them.

"Gabe gave him to me, or he would have died. He is always rescuing people and animals."

"Why don't I make us a cup of tea, and you tell me all about this Gabe. I am assuming he is the one that Joel mentioned who saved you from Reed?" questioned Chad.

Ashley just nodded her head; her headache came back with a vengeance, and her heart felt like it was in pieces. Her brother brought her a cup of steaming hot tea, and just sat there, listening to her tell him all about Gabe. She showed him the web pages and told him about the kid that was sick.

"Well, it seems to me that there is more to this story than a friend just dying," Chad finally said after five minutes of silence.

"You really think that?" asked Ashley, rubbing her temples.

"I do, and I think that if you want some answers, there must be other people you can ask."

"His sister doesn't live far from here, but I can't tell her he is alive."

"And why not? If it was you, then I would want to know."

"Because if he wanted her to know, he would have told her. I can't do that to him."

"Fine, but be careful, and I want to meet this guy soon. Hopefully when he has a house and a job," teased Chad.

Ashley punched her brother in the shoulder and stood up.

"Ouch," cried Chad.

"You know where the blankets are," said Ashley, turning to go.

"And Chad, thank you for not judging."

"No matter what, I will always have your best interests at heart," answered Chad.

Ashley nodded her head and left the room, scooping the kitten into her arms.

The next morning, Ashley woke up with a still-pounding head. She swallowed down some pills and walked into the kitchen to find her brother cooking breakfast.

"Morning, sis, you look tired," said Chad with a grin.

"I am and grumpy too, so be warned."

"How about you go talk to Gabe's sister, and I will get this little kitten here some food and a litter box," replied Chad, handing her a plate of scrambled eggs and toast.

Ashley sat down at the counter, glaring at him as she ate.

"Why are you trying to help me?" asked Ashley suspiciously.

Chad feigned shock at her words, but she knew her brother well.

"How could you ever think I wouldn't help my sister?" "Chad, seriously!"

"Karla is coming over for movies and pizza; her roommates are always in the way," sighed Chad.

"So you want to use my house for your date?"

"Come on, Ash, please just do this for me." pleaded Chad.

"Fine, but when I come back, the dishes should be clean, and you brother dearest should be gone," stated Ashley, putting her empty plate in the sink.

"You are the best," shouted Chad, kissing her on the cheek.

Ashley hurried back to her room and threw on a pair of tight-fitting jeans and a cream-coloured jersey with her ankle boots. She wanted to look good when she met Gabe's family, even if they never knew the real reason why she was there!

Ashley found his sister's address listed, and drove over there. She parked the car and sat there, staring up at the fancy building in front of her. Her nerves were all over the place; part of her felt guilty for going behind Gabe's back. But if he gave her the answers she wanted, she wouldn't need to go look for them herself. With that thought in her mind, Ashley took a deep breath and stepped out of the car. She walked up to the intercom and buzzed the right surname. Ashley was startled out of her deep thoughts by the deep male voice on the other end.

"Hello!" called the voice.

"Yes, Hi, I mean Hello. I am looking for Andrea Snow," said Ashley.

"Who is it that is looking for her?"

"My name is Ashley, and I am a paramedic at the hospital her brother used to work at, and I have a few questions to ask her."

There was silence on the other end for a few seconds, just when Ashley thought that she would get no reply, the door buzzed open. She let out the breath she had been holding and took the lift up to the fifth floor. The doors opened, and a young man with blonde hair and blue eyes stood in an open doorway. Ashley waved and walked towards him; he had a grim look on his face.

"Hi, I am Ashley."

"Luke, and my wife Andy is putting our daughter Gabby down for a nap," said Luke, moving out of the doorway to let her in.

"Gabby?" questioned Ashley.

"Gabriella, named after her uncle Gabriel," answered Luke, ushering her towards the sitting room.

Ashley sat down with her hands in her lap and waited; Luke left the room. She sat there and looked around at all the photos on the wall. Most of them were recent, but there were a few older family ones with Gabe in them. Ashley stood up and walked over to the framed photos; she smiled as she looked at the photos of Gabe and his sister. He looked so carefree in them, nothing like the man she knew now.

"He had just graduated from med school in the picture," said a soft feminine voice from behind.

Ashley gasped and spun around, facing a woman who could be none other than Gabe's sister. She was the female version of him, both striking and beautiful.

Hi, sorry, I wasn't snooping," cried Ashley, making her way back to the chair she had vacated.

"I am Andy, and my husband is making us some tea."

"Thank you." "So why don't you tell me why you are here?"

"I just want to know why Doctor Gabriel Bennett just walked away from everything."

"You didn't ask me if he was alive; you have seen him, haven't you?" cried Andy.

Her eyes filled with tears, and her hands trembled slightly. Luke entered the room at that exact moment and saw his wife's pale complexion. He placed the tray down and, with an angry glare directed at Ashley, he sat down and pulled his wife onto his lap. Ashley smiled at the intimacy the two shared.

"I can't really say."

"I know my brother doesn't want to be found. I just need to know he is alright," said Andy.

"He walked away from being a doctor, and I know he said he killed a patient, I mean a friend, but there must be more to it."

"There is, but I don't know everything. The patient was his best friend Drew; his children were like Gabe's nephews. Drew got really sick, and they said he had a large mass on his brain. He had it removed, but he was paralyzed from the surgery, and a few hours later, he was dead. The same day my brother walked out of that hospital, and I never saw him again," cried Andy.

Ashley held back her tears, thinking about how it must have felt for Gabe to lose his best friend.

"But he thinks he killed him."

"My brother didn't handle the loss well, and he took all the blame on himself. Drew's wife was distraught and lashed out at the first person she saw, who happened to be Gabe. We lost two people that day. One will never come back, and the other, I pray every night that he does," replied Andy.

"I am really sorry for all your loss, but how do you know your brother isn't dead?"

"When Gabby was born, I nearly died, and I was in the hospital for a few days. One night, I saw someone standing over my bed holding Gabby, and I just knew it was my brother."

"He sounds like he was a great guy."

"He was the best, and after our parents died, he took care of me until I met Luke. Ashley, I can see he means something to you. Please try to bring him home to us," pleaded Andy.

"What do you mean?"

"Why would a paramedic be looking for my brother? You are young and beautiful, and I suspect you have come to know my brother well. He is a good guy, and for some reason, he thinks he deserves living the way he does, but he doesn't."

"I really have to go, but thank you for your time. It was nice meeting you," said Ashley.

Gabe stood hidden behind a large dumpster, watching Ashley leave his sister's apartment. His blood boiled as he watched her, feeling hurt that she would go to his family behind his back. What if his sister came looking for him? He stalked towards Ashley's car, knocking loudly on the window. She jumped in fright, before turning to look at him. She wound down the window, guilt written all over her face.

"Why were you at my sister's?" asked Gabe.

"I just wanted some answers, Gabe!" cried Ashley.

"Then you come to me!"

"But you never answer me. I just want to know why. I care about you, Gabe, and I just want to get to know you."

"Don't fool yourself. It is you that you are worried about. How will you tell people that you are dating a homeless guy?" asked Gabe.

"That's not true! I am not ashamed of you! Why can't you see that I am only trying to help?" yelled Ashley.

Gabe opened the car door roughly and peered in at her.

"I am happy with the way I am."

"Then why does your sister think you are dead?"

"Because she deserves better than me. I am a murderer!" shouted Gabe, losing control of his emotions. "You... You just wouldn't understand, Ashley!"

"I don't, and if you explained it, then maybe I would."

"Go home, Ashley, and leave me and my family alone. I don't need you, and I sure as hell don't need your pity," shouted Gabe, slamming the car door shut and walking away.

"But what if I need you?" whispered Ashley to his retreating back.

He stormed off back down the alley, he had been so close to punching a wall or pulling her in for a kiss. He was furious at her for meddling in his life and trying to get him to go back.

He had left for a reason. Gabe walked away from her, refusing to look back. He pulled his collar up and stuck his hands in his pockets, against the chilly air. Gabe strolled aimlessly around for what seemed like hours before going to the one place he hadn't been to in the last few years. The one thing that had started this all!

He walked with purpose through the rows and rows of gravestones, finally stopping in front of the one he wanted. Where the man that had been like a brother to him lay buried! He swallowed past the lump in his throat, staring at the letters of his name. 'Drew Freeman, beloved son, husband, and father'. Gabe glared at the headstone, wishing Drew were alive so that he could shout at him personally.

"You made me promise, and it has taken my life away!" growled Gabe squatting down in front of the headstone.

"I loved you like a brother, and you asked the one thing of me that you knew would ruin me. Why would you do that to me? Why didn't you care to think about me?" sobbed Gabe.

The words blurring as tear drops landed on the ground.

"You knew I would do anything for you; you were my brother," cried Gabe.

Gabe stood up, and without looking back at the gravestone, walked away. Gabe walked back home, feeling raw and unsettled. He had lost Ashley because he hadn't been able to tell her the truth. He was truly alone, and that was what he had always wanted. But suddenly it felt hollow, the reasons for staying away seemed less important now. He missed his sister, his friends, and his home. He missed his old life more than he had ever thought possible.

He took the long way back to the bridge, wanting to see a glimpse of the old life he had once had. He stopped in front of a large white house that looked more like a mansion than a house. The steel gates were chained up, leaving him to stare through at the over grown lawn that once belonged to him. Gabe sighed loudly, his head leaning against the cool bars. The house had been his pride and joy, now it held no appeal.

He turned to leave, when a neighbourhood watch car pulled up in front of him. Gabe stepped back onto the pavement, waiting for the uniformed officer to wind down his window.

"Sir, this is a private residential area, and I am going to have to ask you to leave," said the officer.

"That is my house," stated Gabe, with a thumb pointed over his shoulder.

The officer burst into laughter, shaking his head.

"Yeah, and I am Santa Claus. Now leave before I have you arrested for trespassing!"

Gabe looked back at his house once more before leaving. He strolled along through the area, wondering how he would ever fit in here again. He had seen too much of the other side to ever be able to go back to the way things were before. Gabe shook his head and rubbed his temples, his head throbbing slightly.

He made his way back towards the bridge, but was stopped by a familiar voice calling him. Gabe turned to face Janet, who stood half-leaning against her oldest Chris, while Annie held Mike in her arms. She looked like she was in a lot of pain. Gabe ran a hand through his long hair, his head throbbing worse than before. This was not good; he hadn't seen Janet leave her apartment for a long time.

"Angel Gabe!" shouted Annie excitedly.

Gabe smiled and took the baby from her. Mike clapped his hands and poked Gabe in the nose.

"Nose," said Mike.

"I am so glad I found you, it's Martha. I think she is sick!" cried Janet.

"I don't have any medicine, Janet. I can't just take it all the time," replied Gabe.

"I know, but please just come look," pleaded Janet.

Gabe nodded his head and followed her back towards their building, her movements slow with the help of Chris. Annie took his hand and skipped along next to him as she told him all about her friends. They walked into the building, the heat assaulting him as he entered.

Gabe grimaced and handed Mike back to Annie, who left to go to her apartment with him in her arms. They walked down the passage to the last door on the left. Janet knocked once then pushed open the door. Gabe followed behind her, the apartment was a mess. It looked like it hadn't been cleaned in a while, his stomach rolled over from the smell alone. Gabe held his breath and followed Janet down the little passage and into the dark room. Seventy-five-year-old, Martha was lying on her bed looking pale and sweaty. Gabe walked past Janet and her son and approached the bed.

"Hello, Martha," said Gabe.

"Angel Gabriel, I haven't seen you for a while," cried Martha weakly.

"Janet says you aren't feeling too well," replied Gabe softly.

"She shouldn't have called you, I am fine. Nothing a bit of bed rest can't cure," laughed Martha.

"Humour me, show me what is wrong, and if it is nothing, I will leave."

She hesitated for a few seconds before slowly drawing back the blanket to reveal her right arm. Gabe swallowed back the bile rising in his throat as he looked down at the bandaged arm. The smell was stronger without the blankets, the bandage a yellow colour.

"May I take a look?" asked Gabe.

She nodded her head, biting her lip nervously.

"It was just a small insect bite that wouldn't go away," cried Martha, closing her eyes.

Gabe unravelled the dirty cloth and held back from cursing at the sight of the infested wound covered in maggots. He heard Janet gasp behind him and told Chris to leave with his mother.

"Martha, your wound has become infected," said Gabe.

"I was scared to leave the house," sobbed Martha, refusing to look at the wound.

Gabe placed the cloth over it and paced back and forth.

"I need to call an ambulance; you need surgery to clean out the wound," said Gabe.

"No! Please don't do that," sobbed Martha.

"I don't have the right stuff to flush out the infection, Martha. I can take the maggots out, but you need real help."

"Just do what you can."

Gabe groaned in frustration and walked out of the room. He put a bowl of boiling water and a clean cloth on the table next to her bed and found a pair of tweezers.

Gabe switched on the overhead light and told Martha to close her eyes for a bit. She nodded her head, and he sat down on the edge of the bed. Gabe slowly removed every maggot from the wound before cleaning it out and re-bandaging the clean wound. By the time he was done, he was sweating profusely.

"Alright, Martha, it is clean. Now I need you to keep cleaning this with warm water, or maggots will be the least of your worries," said Gabe.

"Thank you," cried Martha.

Gabe made her a cup of tea and left the apartment.

Once outside, he stripped off his jacket. He felt slightly hot, and his stomach was a little unsettled. Gabe ran a hand through his wet hair and made his way towards the bathrooms. He found an empty shower stall in the public gym bathrooms and a bar of soap. He found an empty shower stall in the public gym bathrooms and a bar of soap. He stood under the cold water and scrubbed his skin raw, until the feeling of crawling maggots washed away with the soap. He dressed himself, his head spinning slightly, and made his way back to the bridge. Gabe sat down against a pillar, shivering slightly. He knew he had a fever and that he needed help, but he was exhausted and just wanted to sleep for a while. He closed his eyes, his arms wrapped around his body, and sank into an exhausted sleep.

CHAPTER 10

Ashley stood watching Evan lying in his hospital bed with earbuds in his ears as he listened to music. She watched him tap his fingers to the beat of the music.

"I see you have taken a shine to my patient," said Zack.

Ashley jumped slightly, placing a hand over her beating heart. Turning to face Zack, who was standing behind her.

"You scared me, Doctor!" cried Ashley.

"Sorry, what are you doing here, Ash?" "I came to see if you found a way to help Evan."

"I told you there is no one qualified to do that type of surgery," replied Zack sadly.

"And if by some small chance Gabriel Bennett were to come back, would he be able to do it?" asked Ashley.

Zack stared at her, his arms crossed as he eyed her suspiciously.

"What do you know that I don't?" questioned Zack.

"Nothing, I was just wondering," answered Ashley.

"Well, there is no use wondering. Yes, if Gabe was around he could do the surgery, but that is impossible."

Their conversation was interrupted. Suddenly Ashley's radio crackled before Romeo called her for an emergency. Ashley said goodbye to Zack and ran towards her partner. He sat in the ambulance, the engine running as Ashley hopped in. They followed the directions towards the bridge, her heart beating faster and faster the closer they got. The ambulance came to a stop, and Ashley jumped out, running towards the very familiar man slumped over.

"What happened?" asked Ashley, kneeling in front of him.

"He sat up, and then he just vomited. Afterwards, he collapsed again and wouldn't wake up," said someone.

Ashley looked down at Gabe, her heart beating erratically. Romeo approached them with the medic bag. Ashley gave him a grateful smile and quickly checked Gabe's rising temperature.

"His temperature is really high. He could be dehydrated.," cried Ashley.

Romeo helped her strap him to the board and wheeled him to the ambulance. Ashley sat in the back checking his vitals. Suddenly, Gabe grabbed her wrist, his eyes flying open. "

No hospital," groaned Gabe.

"You could be dying. I have to," cried Ashley.

"No, just food poisoning," croaked Gabe, grabbing his stomach.

"Gabe! I have to, please!"

"No! Please don't make me go back there," pleaded Gabe, staring straight into her eyes.

Ashley swallowed then turned to look at Romeo.

"Romeo! Go to my apartment."

"What?" yelled Romeo!

"Just do it! He knows what is wrong with himself, and if he gets worse, I will take him myself," stated Ashley, combing a hand through his hair.

"Are you mad? We could both get fired over this," cried Romeo.

"He won't die, please, Romeo."

"How do you know that?"

"Because he is a doctor. Now please. I will call in sick and stay to take care of him," begged Ashley.

"Fine, but you owe me big time," groaned Romeo, making a U-turn.

Together, they were able to get Gabe up the stairs and into her apartment. Ashley laid him on her bed and pulled off his shoes before throwing them aside. She placed a bucket next to the bed and a glass of water. Romeo stood in the doorway, watching her with a concerned look on his face.

"Are you sure you will be alright?" asked Romeo.

"Yes, just go and tell them that it was a prank call. I will see you soon," whispered Ashley as she pulled a blanket over Gabe.

He shivered slightly before curling into a ball. She waited for Romeo to leave before calling in sick.

Gabe groaned and rolled over, the sun burning his eyes. He pulled the blanket over his head, his empty stomach grumbling out loud.

"Seems like you are feeling better?" said Ashley.

Gabe threw the blanket off himself and sat up. He was in Ashley's bed, in her apartment. He looked around the room, finding Ashley sitting in a chair reading a book.

"What happened?" croaked Gabe, his throat dry and scratchy.

She stood up and handed him a glass of water.

"You were very sick," answered Ashley.

Gabe drank the whole glass of water, handing it back to her. He looked down at his bare chest and back up at Ashley.

"How long have I been out for?" asked Gabe.

"Almost three days, your fever broke yesterday," answered Ashley.

Gabe remembered waking a few times disoriented. He remembered throwing up continuously and being helped to the bathroom a few times. He looked straight at Ashley.

"You took care of me! Why?"

"Someone needed to," shrugged Ashley, lifting the black kitten off his lap and into her arms.

"I slept in your bed."

"I know, I couldn't let you sleep in the sitting room as sick as you were," replied Ashley.

Gabe turned and placed his bare feet onto the floor. He lifted his shirt off the floor and slipped it over his head.

"I see you kept the kitten."

"Yes, I named him Ninja," smiled Ashley.

Gabe nodded his head, staring at her intensely.

"Thank you for helping, I know I've been a bit distant and cold towards you. I really don't deserve your help, Ashley," said Gabe.

"Everyone needs someone to care about them, Gabe. I might not always understand you, but I do care. Now I really have to go to work, so I will see you later?" replied Ashley, leaving the room.

Gabe stared at the closed bedroom door, long after she was gone.

His stomach grumbled out loud, and he stood up on weak legs, pulling on his shoes and heading out the door. He found a sandwich on the counter and ate it hungrily. He took a quick shower, then left a note for Ashley and left her apartment.

He stood outside in the sun, stretching his muscles and walked off. He barely remembered the last few days, delirious from the fever. But he remembered Ashley's soft hands running across his inflamed body and her soothing voice talking to him. He hadn't felt that cared for in a long time. He scratched at his beard, he hadn't shaven in a few days, and walked towards the bridge. He knew they would be worried about him. What people didn't know was that they cared for each other on the streets. He stepped under the bridge and for the first time in a long time, he felt uneasy about being here. He felt out of place and a little lost. Gabe searched the mostly empty area, but most people had started their day already. He suddenly remembered Martha and her wound and hurried towards the apartments where she stayed. He stopped outside the building, slightly out of breath and weak from his recent recovery. Two ambulances were parked out front. A gurney was wheeled out with a white sheet covering the person. Gabe pushed through the crowds of people gathering, spotting Janet with her husband and children to one side.

"What happened?" asked Gabe.

Janet turned towards him, her cheeks tear-stained.

"We couldn't find you... She died!"

Gabe stepped back at the force of anger Janet was directing towards him.

"Who died?" asked Gabe.

"Martha, they said she had blood poisoning," sobbed Janet.

"I am so sorry, I was sick the last few days," answered Gabe.

"She just died," said her husband Lenny.

Gabe swallowed and stepped back, the pain in these people's eyes raw as an open wound. He turned and ran away. He had failed to help them. He ran and ran until he reached the one place he could be alone to think.

Ashley walked into her empty apartment, picked up the note Gabe had left, and smiled at his scribbled thank-you note. She was worried about him. Today, a call had come in about an old woman dying from blood poisoning in the old apartment building Gabe had taken her to. Ashley changed into jeans and a blue hooded shirt, then packed a light picnic hamper and left her apartment. She drove towards the bridge, seeing that Gabe wasn't be there, before heading to the junkyard. She parked her car, took out her backpack, and slipped through the hole in the fence. Ashley walked through the abandoned junkyard, searching for Gabe.

"Gabe, are you here?" Ashley called out.

"What are you doing here?" yelled Gabe. Ashley turned around and looked up.

Gabe sat lounging in his usual chair. He portrayed a man relaxing, but she could see the turmoil in his eyes.

"I brought us food," answered Ashley, climbing up the junk pile.

She nearly slipped, but a hand grabbed hers and pulled her up. She looked up at Gabe and smiled.

"You shouldn't be here, Ashley," said Gabe.

"I heard about Martha, and I am really sorry," replied Ashley, gently touching his cheek.

He pulled away and slumped back into the chair.

"Don't be, she was just an old woman living in an apartment," grumbled Gabe, staring past her.

"If it makes you feel better to shrug it off, then that's what you will do. But I won't let you do it alone," said Ashley, pulling open her bag and handing him an apple.

He took it from her, pulling the spare chair forward so that she could sit down next to him. Ashley smiled and sat down next to him, biting into her own apple. "Am I in time for the sunset?" asked Ashley.

"Yes, ma'am," smiled Gabe, biting into his own apple. They sat together eating the food silently as they watched the sunset.

A week later, Ashley and Romeo were on their way to an accident on the bridge. A truck had burst its tire and drove into three cars before tipping over and losing its cargo on another two. There were multiple victims, a few dead and others still trapped. Ashley got out of the ambulance and ran towards the closest car. It was on its side with the front windshield shattered. She peered inside to see a woman pinned to her seat with a metal rod through her arm.

"I have a metal rod through her arm here; she is unconscious with a bump to the head," called Ashley.

Suddenly, a shadow passed over her, and she looked up into Gabe's face.

"Are you here to help or watch?" asked Ashley.

"Help," answered Gabe. Ashley smiled and yanked open the car door. She leaned back out and stuck her hand out towards Gabe.

"Gabe, you will need this," said Ashley, handing him a hairband.

He flashed her a smile and tied his hair up, before moving on to the next vehicle. Ashley gently touched the woman's shoulder.

"Ma'am, I am a paramedic. Can you hear me?" asked Ashley, shining a torch in her eyes.

"I see your boy is helping today," shouted Romeo from the next car. Ashley ignored his comment and carried on working.

"I need to remove the rod from her arm, Romeo!" replied Ashley.

My baby! Where is my baby?" murmured the woman.

Ashley peered in the back of the car, and the car seat was empty.

"Romeo, there is a small child somewhere; the seat is empty."

"Where is my baby?" screamed the frantic woman, yanking the rod out of her arm.

Blood started squirting out of her arm, and Ashley dived forward, sticking her fingers inside the hole.

"She has an artery bleed," yelled Ashley.

The woman fought Ashley off, and Ashley pinned her down with her weight.

"If you don't keep still, you will bleed out, and then you won't be any good to your child," commanded Ashley.

"Kyle, his name is Kyle, and he is only three-years-old. He must be so scared," sobbed the woman.

"We will look for Kyle. What is your name?"

"Donna, please find my baby." Ashley nodded her head and pulled her radio loose.

"I need backup here; we have a ruptured artery," stated Ashley.

Suddenly, Gabe appeared through the other side, slipping his fingers next to hers in the hole. Ashley looked up at his stern expression.

"Leave her to me. I know what to do. Go find that child," said Gabe.

Ashley nodded her head and slipped her fingers out as smoothly as Gabe slipped his in. The woman hissed and cried out in pain. Ashley stood up and searched the smoke and wreckage for the toddler.

"Kyle... Kyle... Where are you?" shouted Ashley, peering under cars for the little boy.

She climbed on top of the overturned truck and searched the area for the little boy. Ashley jumped down and ran between cars, checking the other ambulances for the kid. She turned to head back to the car when she heard a small whimper. Ashley ran towards the sound, her heart beating faster the closer she got. She searched the area, ready to give up when a squeaky noise came from under her foot. She looked down at the teddy bear and picked it up, walking towards the edge of the bridge and peering over the edge. She tried to stay calm and not panic, going over her training in her head as she watched the little boy sitting on the edge of a cement slab hanging over the edge. His chubby face was covered in black soot and tears.

The truck must have lost a cement slab over the edge, and it was jammed into the structure of the bridge.

"Kyle? My name is Ashley, and I am a paramedic," said Ashley cautiously approaching the cement slab.

The boy looked up at her with stunning blue eyes, clutching his little bloody arm to his chest.

"I want my mommy; I have a sore," sobbed Kyle.

"I know, sweetie, and your mommy wants you," replied Ashley.

She looked around at the fire department putting out a fire and at the boy, who was suddenly standing up on the cement slab.

"NO! Kyle! Stay right where you are," screamed Ashley.

She lifted her radio up.

"I need back up now, the south end of the bridge. A child is balancing on a piece of cement, and I don't know how much longer he can wait," cried Ashley.

She looked up at the boy who had taken one wobbly step closer.

"Kyle, please don't move. I am going to get a rope and come and get you," said Ashley.

He shook his head of blonde curls and took another step forward.

Where is that ladder?" shouted Ashley into her radio.

"We are on our way, keep him there," replied the voice.

"My arm hurts, it's bleeding," sobbed Kyle, taking another step closer.

Ashley knew that there was no chance of him waiting. If she waited for the ladder, he would die. She slowly climbed up onto the ledge, her limbs shaking.

"Ashley, get down!" yelled Gabe.

She drowned out all the voices behind her and crawled onto the cement slab. It creaked and swayed forward. Ashley lurched forward, grabbing onto the sides. Kyle fell down onto his hands and knees, crying.

"Kyle! Look at me, I have your teddy bear and he misses you," whispered Ashley, slowly crawling a few steps forward.

Kyle attempted to stand up again, but nearly fell over the side.

"NO!" screamed Ashley.

"I want to go home," cried Kyle.

"I know, sweetie. I need you to slow crawl to me," replied Ashley.

"Ashley, you will kill yourself, come back," yelled Gabe.

Ashley bit her lip and stretched out her hand. Kyle stretched out his in return, his tongue between his teeth. The cement slab let out another groan and shifted again, causing them both to lurch forward. Ashley watched in slow motion as Kyle slipped over the side. She slid forward and grabbed him by his shirt collar.

"Do not let anyone touch this or it will fall," screamed Ashley, pulling Kyle up into her arms.

He latched onto her, wrapping his legs around her waist. She sat with a leg on either side.

"Don't let go, Kyle," said Ashley, slowly turning around.

A crowd was forming on the bridge, all watching her with the boy. A group of firemen stood by the railing along with Gabe. Ashley took a deep breath and slowly inched forward on her bum, the little boy trembling in her arms. She was in touching distance of the railing. A fireman stood up onto the railing and stretched out his arm. Ashley grabbed onto his arm and let him pull her up and over the railing. A cheer erupted in the crowd around them,. Ashley swayed to the side, unsteady on her feet. A pair of strong arms wrapped around her, pulling her against a flat chest. She turned and looked at Gabe, his eyes filled with raw emotions.

"I want my mommy," sobbed Kyle.

Ashley looked down at the boy in her arms, giving him a weak smile. She walked with the boy in her arms, through the crowd, Gabe's arm still around her. The ambulance came into view, and Donna sat inside, her face lighting up at the sight of her son.

"Kyle!" screamed Donna.

"Mommy," yelled Kyle, squirming out of Ashley's arms and into his mother's.

Ashley left the two alone for a few minutes, her body still shaking from adrenaline. She turned around and nearly walked straight into Gabe. She looked up and swallowed. He was covered in blood, and his shirt was torn, but his eyes were filled with emotions she wasn't sure she could handle right now.

He gripped her elbow gently and steered her around the side of the ambulance, away from prying eyes. Gabe pushed her gently against the side, his hands running all over her. She felt the tremble in his hands and looked up into his stormy eyes. Ashley grabbed his hands in hers and brought them to her lips. She kissed them gently before placing them over her heart.

"I am fine."

"You could have died," Gabe replied with a slight tremble.

"He would have died if I didn't go out there."

"Don't ever do that again," stated Gabe, leaving no room for argument.

"Not if someone needs..." started Ashley, but was cut off with Gabe's lips on hers.

His lips were soft and gentle against hers. She moaned slightly and pulled him closer.

"Ashley, we need to go," called Romeo, starting the ambulance.

Gabe pulled away, staring down at her with an intensity that scared her in a good way, before turning and walking away.

CHAPTER 11

Gabe stepped back into the shadows, watching his sister climb out of a taxi with Annabel Freeman. Both women looked happy and carefree, dressed smartly in cocktail dresses. They paid the driver and turned to face Ashley's building.

"Are you sure it is alright for the boys and me to sleep here tonight?" asked Annabel.

"Of course, Luke phoned to say they are asleep with Gabby in her room. You don't want to wake them now and make the trip home alone, do you?" replied Andy, digging in her purse for her keys.

Before Annabel could reply, a hooded figure turned the corner, stepping in front of them. Gabe took a step forward, his fists clenching.

"Well, well, well. What do we have here? Two ladies alone in the night," said the man.

"We live right here, and my husband knows I am outside, so please just go," cried Andy.

"I only see us three here alone," replied the man, swinging his hands around to encompass the whole street.

"I will scream if you don't go, and this building is filled with people who will hear me and come help," declared Andy.

"Please just leave us, we have children," sobbed Annabel.

"I don't want to hurt you, I just want a little bit of cash." "We don't have any."

"Now that is a shame, ladies, because if I have to walk away with nothing, then I might not be able to control myself, and when I don't get my own way, I get violent."

"No! Please don't," begged Andy.

He stepped closer, trailing his dirty finger along her cheek. Gabe watched her shudder with disgust and stepped fully out of the shadows.

"Leave them alone!" commanded Gabe.

The man, clearly surprised, turned to face Gabe. Andy saw her chance and kneed him between the legs. He turned and grabbed her wrist, squeezing it painfully.

"I will cut you into pieces," growled the man in pain.

Gabe walked up to him and grabbed him by the neck, squeezing hard.

"Let her go before I crush your throat," growled Gabe.

"Alright, just let go," whispered the man, his voice raspy from the pressure.

"You first," spat Gabe.

He let go of Andy, and Gabe shoved him away. He followed behind the man, until he turned the corner and out of sight. The door opened behind them, and Luke stepped out, quickly approaching Andy and checking her for any injuries.

"What happened? I looked out the window and saw him harassing you," cried Luke.

"He was, but we were saved," replied Andy.

Gabe stalked back into the shadows, keeping an eye on the guy as he slunk away.

He turned to face his sister, watching her being cradled in her husband's arms.

"Who saved you?" questioned Luke, searching the deserted area.

"I think it was my brother," whispered Andy, shaking slightly.

"Gabe is alive!" cried Annabel, her eyes searching for the man that had killed her husband.

"Yes, Gabe is alive," answered Andy, opening the apartment door.

"Then why doesn't he come home?" asked Annabel.

"Maybe you should be telling me why," replied Andy, with a helpless shrug.

"It isn't my story to tell, I just wish he would let me say I am sorry," answered Annabel, closing the door.

Gabe stood with his back against the wall, the bricks cold and hard against his head. Why would Annabel need to say sorry? He was the one that had killed her husband. He was the one that had destroyed both their lives. He was no better than that guy that had tried to rob them; he could try to do good, but under it all, he was as bad as them all. With a frustrated sigh, he zipped up his jacket and walked away from his sister once more. Gabe found himself outside Ashley's building, staring up at her window, the lights still on inside. He should just walk away now and leave her be, but just the thought of seeing her made the cold places in his heart light up. He approached the intercom, his finger hovering over the button as he thought of the many reasons why this was a bad idea. With a sad, self-mocking laugh, he pushed the buzzer.

"Hello!" called Ashley. "Hey, Ashley, it's me, Gabe," replied Gabe.

"Oh, hey, Gabe, I just finished eating. Do you want to come up for a cup of coffee?" questioned Ashley.

"I was hoping that you would come down here and come with me," said Gabe, holding his breath as he waited for a reply.

"Sure, let me just put on my shoes, and I will be right down," stated Ashley.

Gabe stuck his hands in his pockets, turning to stare at all the modern houses around him. He heard the door open behind him and peered over his shoulder. She stood on the front steps shyly, snuggled in a large black coat.

"So where are we going?" asked Ashley.

"I want to show you my world," answered Gabe, holding out his hand. He watched her stare at his hand in the dark, before taking a step forward and slipping her hand in his.

Gabe smiled and pulled her closer. She let out a small gasp, trying to stop herself from falling. He laughed and wrapped his arms around her and dipped down, kissing her gently on the lips.

"Hmm, what was that for?" asked Ashley, her lips inches from his.

"I missed you," replied Gabe, stepping back and taking her hand in his again.

He strolled with her down the street, keeping to the light. His usual need for darkness, faded around her. Gabe led her through the streets and to the back of the shopping mall and found an old trolley just lying there. He smiled and let go of Ashley's hand, so that he could grab onto it.

"What are you doing?" cried Ashley.

"Giving you a true homeless night," smiled Gabe, pushing the trolley out of the parking area.

"And what is that supposed to mean?" questioned Ashley skeptically.

"Get in the trolley and I will show you," she said.

She stared at the trolley, then back at Gabe, his smile like that of a boy on Christmas day.

"But it is dark," cried Ashley.

"Then let me take you to the light," said Gabe with a gestured wave of his hand towards the lit pathway leading to the park.

Ashley rolled her eyes and climbed into the trolley, sitting with her back to Gabe. He leaned forward and whispered in her ear.

"Hold on." Gabe grabbed the handle of the trolley and took off running through the parking area and towards the park.

The evening breeze blew their hair back as he whisked along the pathways. Ashley held on, laughing happily. Gabe chuckled to himself and picked up the pace.

"I hope you know how to drive this?" teased Ashley, her cheeks flushed.

"Yup, graduated in Trolley steering school with an A," replied Gabe in a serious tone.

She threw back her head and laughed. Gabe slowed down the trolley as he laughed in return. It had been so long since he had such fun. He stopped the trolley in front of the lake under a street lamp and stared at Ashley.

"That was a lot of fun," said Ashley.

"Yeah, it was. I guess we both just needed to have a carefree moment."

"I know what you mean. Thank you for not being ashamed of who you are and for showing me your world." Gabe smiled and held out his hand.

Ashley took it and let him help her to the ground. They sat down on the semi-wet grass, watching the moon reflect on the surface of the lake. They sat in content silence, Gabe's arm around Ashley. She looked over at him. He had on a clean grey shirt that made his eyes look brighter and a much newer pair of jeans. He kept his face clean-shaven. She had the urge to run her fingers along his jaw. Instead, she stopped staring at him and looked back at the water in front of them. After a few minutes, she began to shiver. Gabe peered down at her and sighed. He wanted to stay here all night, but he knew she needed to get warm.

"Come on, we have one more stop to make," said Gabe, standing up.

Ashley felt more alive tonight, being with Gabe, than she had in a very long time. She took his hand and let him lead her, trusting him to keep her safe. She had been taught that after dark, you stayed inside where it was safe. But for Gabe, it was the opposite. He led her towards the bridge, and she wasn't sure what to expect this time of night. They turned the corner, and the bridge came into view. Ashley saw a few drums with fires inside of them under the bridge, with people surrounding them. Gabe led them to one with a few spots open. Gabe led her to one of the drums. The warmth coming from the drum hit her in an instant. She stepped forward and held her hands close to the drum, copying what the others were doing. Gabe stepped closer behind her, and she smiled and stepped back into him.

She felt him relax slightly as he wrapped his arms around her waist.

"These are my people," whispered Gabe.

"Who do you have there, Gabe? She sure is pretty and doesn't look like one of us," said a small guy opposite her.

"This is my girlfriend Ashley. Ashley, these are some of my friends. That there is Magpie," said Gabe, pointing to the man that had just spoken.

He waved in return, showing her a smile with missing teeth.

"Then next to him is Runner, he is the fastest man around," whispered Gabe, pointing to the tall guy with dreadlocks standing next to her.

"And lastly, this here is Lady Bess, she is like the mother we all lost," smiled Gabe, pointing to a large older woman standing on the other side of them.

"Hello, everyone," said Ashley, waving.

"Why are you bringing someone like her here? It isn't safe," cried Lady Bess.

"I trust Gabe to keep me safe; he saved me once already," said Ashley, placing her arms over his.

"Angel Gabriel is everyone's hero," stated Runner happily.

"I am just an ordinary guy," shrugged Gabe.

"Do you mind me asking how you all ended up here?" asked Ashley.

They all let out a weary sigh, the sparkle in their eyes dimming a bit.

"I am a mom, you know, have four grown kids and who knows how many grandkids. But I was selfish, and I chose another man over my husband, I chose drugs, and in the end, it destroyed me and my family. I lost everything. I finally hit rock bottom after I nearly overdosed, and by then I had no one to care about me. I had no job experiences, married straight out of high school, and so I found it easier to be here. I figured that if I needed to be punished for my sins, what better place than to live here on the streets," said Lady Bess.

"That is so sad, but surely your kids would want you home?"

I don't deserve them; I deserted them, and they are better off without me."

Ashley wanted to tell her otherwise, but Gabe squeezed her arm softly. She looked up at him, and he shook his head slightly.

"My story isn't so glamorous; I lost my job ten years ago and basically I couldn't find another one. Soon I had nowhere besides the streets," told Runner.

"But they said you were fast. Why not pursue running?"

"I had a full track scholarship, and I blew it by getting a DUI after a party one night," sighed Runner.

"My turn, little lady, my real name is Tristan Jeremiah the third, and I was the CEO of TRIM Designs seven years ago .I had the fastest cars, a house, and everything I could ever want. I was selfish and arrogant, and I was blind to my partner's schemes. He took me for all that I was worth, tried to get me arrested, and I ran, and I have been hiding here ever since," replied Magpie.

"Wow, hearing your stories make me really feel selfish for everything I have."

"And you, missy, what are you doing here with our Gabe?"

She felt Gabe tense behind her slightly. Ashley gave his arm a light squeeze.

"I like Gabe the way he is; he is sweet and caring and like all of you said. He is a hero, my hero," said Ashley.

"I see love in your eyes," smiled Lady Bess.

Ashley blushed under all the scrutiny. Gabe cleared his throat behind her.

"We should be getting you home; it's getting late," said Gabe, his voice sounding rough from the raw intensity of his emotions.

"Thank you for sharing your stories with me, and I am really sorry your life turned out the way it has," said Ashley.

"Don't be; some of us needed this. It opened our eyes and gave us a chance to redeem ourselves in our own eyes. Because if you can't look at yourself in the mirror, then how can you look at anyone else."

She smiled, feeling heartbroken for these people, and waved one last time before letting Gabe lead her back home.

Ashley hadn't seen much of Gabe in the last week; she had been working late shifts and going home just to sleep. She hadn't heard much from her brothers recently and was slightly worried about her father. She had another late shift tonight, and as usual, Romeo was driving, but he looked no less exhausted than she did. Ashley yawned and rubbed her eyes. The radio beeped, and they were told that a lady was going crazy in a 24/7 corner shop not far from where they were now. Ashley hated these types of calls because they sometimes got out of hand. They parked the ambulance outside the store, and the owner stood on the sidewalk looking distressed.

"She is crazy, you have to help," cried the man.

"We'll go in, check it out, and then decide," said Romeo.

She took a deep breath as she heard the woman's frantic screams coming through the open door. Ashley followed Romeo inside; he held out his hand to stop her from getting closer. The woman looked to be in her late forties with dishevelled hair and messy clothing. Her eyes were bloodshot and wild.

"Stay away from me! It is dangerous," screamed the woman.

"Ma'am, we are paramedics, and we are here to help you," called Romeo.

"You can't help me, no one can," yelled the woman, knocking shelves over.

"What is wrong with her?" asked the shop owner.

"Looks like she is high on bath salts; people tend to smoke it these days," said Ashley, opening the medical bag.

"Give me 2ml midazolam; let's incapacitate her before she does any more harm," stated Romeo.

Ashley took out the injection and filled it, then cautiously approached the lady.

"Ma'am, we want to help you."

"No, the voices are bad, evil, and I have to make them stop!" screamed the woman, pulling a gun out of her back pocket.

"Call the police now!" yelled Romeo, lifting his radio up and signalling for backup.

"We can help you, just put down the gun and let us help make the voices stop," soothed Ashley, slowly taking a step closer.

"Ash, stop! Don't move!" said Romeo.

The woman spun to face Ashley, her hand shaking with the gun in it.

"You are lying to me, stop lying," shouted the woman, waving the gun around.

"Alright, I am sorry. But let's just talk for a bit. My name is Ashley, and you are?"

"No, no, don't listen to them. They just want to get into your head and lie to you. Ssshh," stated the woman, smacking her own head with the side of the gun.

"Ash, back down now, walk slowly towards me," yelled Romeo.

Ashley took one step backward, the woman screamed and lunged for Ashley. She dropped the injection onto the floor.

"No, I won't let you stop me," growled the woman, squeezing Ashley's arm tightly.

Ashley bit back the cry of pain as the dirty nails dug into her flesh. The woman waved the gun in Ashley's face.

"You can't stop me! No one can!" "Ma'am, please let go of my partner," pleaded Romeo.

"Lies, lies, just shut up and let me think," screamed the woman. "It's going to be alright, just give me the gun, and we can walk out of here together," begged Ashley.

"No! I need to finish this. I need to stop her before she kills again," stammered the woman, lifting the gun.

"NO!" screamed Romeo, lunging forward.

Ashley closed her eyes as the gun went off.

CHAPTER 12

Ashley opened her eyes just as Romeo tackled her to the ground. She looked down at the gruesome matter all over her. Her mind was reeling; she could barely think.

"Ash! Ash! Are you alright?" repeated Romeo.

"What happened?" croaked Ashley.

"She stopped the voices in her head," answered Romeo.

Ashley nodded her head, slowly standing up on shaky feet. She felt nauseous thinking about all the brain matter on her. She just wanted to get clean but knew that there would be a whole bunch of paperwork and questions. Her stomach rolled at the sight of what was left of the woman's head. She ran past Romeo, bending over to vomit into a trash can on the side of the street. Once her stomach had emptied, she lifted her hand to wipe her mouth, seeing blood on her hand and bent over to vomit again. Ashley lifted her head up, a bottle of fresh water was lifted towards her mouth. She drank from it slowly, staring past it at Gabe. Romeo walked out of the shop, talking on his radio. In the distance, they could hear police cars approaching. "Thank you," stammered Ashley, shivering slightly.

"I called it in, Ash. They want to question us after we get cleaned up. Someone is coming to relieve us, and then we can go back to New Port Memorial Hospital," said Romeo.

Ashley nodded her head as she was unable to say anything.

"I am going with for the ride!" stated Gabe.

Romeo stared at Gabe, looked at her, and then nodded.

Back at the hospital, she let Gabe take her hand and lead her towards the staff bathrooms.

"Let's get you cleaned up a bit," said Gabe.

He walked her over to a shower stall and turned the taps on. Gabe checked the temperature and turned to face Ashley.

"I will go wait outside," said Gabe.

"Don't leave me," pleaded Ashley.

"I asked Romeo to get you clean clothing from your locker, just stand in there with your clothes on," replied Gabe.

Ashley nodded her head, closing her eyes and stepping inside. She kept them closed as she let the matter run off her. After a minute or two, she opened her eyes and looked down at her still red hands. Ashley picked up a scrubbing brush and began scrubbing her hands raw. She wanted it all off, she became frantic when it wouldn't come off. Tears streaming down her cheeks as she slid to the floor with a loud thump.

"Ashley, are you alright?" called Gabe.

"It won't come off!" sobbed Ashley.

The curtain opened, and Gabe stepped into the shower fully clothed; he let the water soak him wet as he knelt down in front of Ashley.

Gabe gently pulled her hands away from her chest and picked up the bar of soap, scrubbing her fingers clean. Ashley stared at his large hands cleaning hers, tears running down her cheeks.

"I couldn't save her," mumbled Ashley.

He looked up at her and pulled her into his arms.

"We can't save them all," whispered Gabe, holding her tight.

They sat there for a few seconds, both fully clothed as the water ran clean down the drain.

"Ash, I brought you some clothing," called Karla.

Gabe stood up slowly, pulling her to her feet with him. He shut the water off and pulled open the curtain. Ashley stepped out of the shower, looking over her shoulder at Gabe, his hair plastered to his cheeks and his clothing hanging on him. Karla stepped into view with a towel and wrapped it around her, leading her away. Gabe walked out of the bathrooms, where Romeo stood in clean clothing, holding out a pair of scrubs for Gabe. He took them and walked back inside, quickly pulling them on. He looked down at himself in the blue scrubs, the last time he had worn one had been when he had killed his best friend. He gathered up his wet clothing and left the hospital.

Gabe walked down to Ashley's apartment building, sitting outside on the steps as he waited for her to come home. An hour later, she stood next to him and without a word opened the door and led them inside.

"Why don't you make us some coffee, while I put our wet clothing in the dryer," said Ashley, her back to Gabe.

He gently pulled her round to face him, moving her hair out of her face.

"When the coffee is done, I want to tell you why I left," replied Gabe.

Her eyes widened in surprise, she nodded and took his clothing from him. Gabe made them coffee and placed it on the coffee table before sitting down and stretching out his legs. Ashley would be the first person he had ever told this story to, and he knew that there was the possibility of her hating him afterward, but she needed to know. She came back into the room in sweats and a baggy top, cautiously approaching. Gabe held out his hand, and she took it. He pulled her down onto his lap. He waited for her to get comfortable, wrapping his arms around her.

"After I tell you this, you might not want me to ever touch you again," said Gabe sadly.

"Let me be the one to decide that!" Gabe nodded his head, wondering where to start.

He dropped his head onto her shoulder, and she moved her arm around him, so that she could run her fingers through his hair.

"Drew and I were like brothers; we grew up together. We did everything together, even studied at the same university. But Drew wanted to be an accountant while I wanted to be a doctor. Throughout college, we were inseparable. Drew had lost his parents when he was fourteen and had moved in with us. He was truly my brother and was just as devastated when my parents died. He married Annabel, and together they had two boys, Davie and Cullum. About four years ago, Drew got sick; he collapsed at work," said Gabe.

"He had a tumour, didn't he?" asked Ashley sympathetically.

"Yes, he did," croaked Gabe, his voice breaking with emotions.

"He got very sick, and after many tests, surgery was the only answer. But the surgery was dangerous and could leave him paralyzed from the head down. Without it, he would die, and with it, he would have a small chance of recovery. So I did the surgery."

"And he died?"

"No, but there were serious complications, and he was left paralyzed from the neck down. I had made him a promise, and it was one I wished I had never made."

"What did you promise, Gabe?" asked Ashley.

"I...I promised to kill him if he became paralyzed," answered Gabe, releasing her.

She turned around and straddled his lap, lifting his chin up so he could look into his eyes.

"Why?"

"You tell me what you would have done if your best friend begged you to not let him live as a vegetable, to not let his sons see him like that. I didn't want to, but he meant everything to me, and he wouldn't stop until I said yes," cried Gabe.

"So what did you do?" "I kept my promise. I made it look like I had made a mistake in the operating room, and he bled out. His wife looked straight at me after the surgery and said I killed him. I have his blood on my hands."

"Oh, Gabe! If he truly loved you as a brother, he should never have asked that of you!" cried Ashley, wrapping her arms around him.

"Just stop, I am a monster. Don't you see, I took an oath, and I broke that by killing my best friend. How can I ever be a doctor again?"

"I think you have paid enough over the years for what you did."

"How can you look at me after I told you I killed someone?" asked Gabe.

"Because the man I know did what he did for someone else and suffered for it. The way I see it, you both died in that operating room that day, and Drew won't be ever coming back. But you still have that option, Gabe! It was a pretty selfless act if you ask me."

Gabe felt small tremors run through his body as he cried while Ashley held him and just let him have his moment. Afterwards, they lay together on the two-seater and watched movies until they fell asleep.

Ashley awoke to the sun slowly peeking through the half-closed blinds, her head felt fuzzy and she barely remembered falling asleep. The movement under her, alerted her to the fact that she had fallen asleep on Gabe. She quickly jumped off of him, her face blood red from embarrassment. He rolled over in his sleep, his features looking more relaxed after last night's confession. She quickly took a shower and put on clean clothing, taking Gabe's clothes out of the dryer. On her return to the sitting room, she found Gabe awake. She handed him the clothes.

"Go shower quickly, I want to take you somewhere," said Ashley.

He arched a brow in question. She laughed and placed her hands on her hips.

"Don't give me that look, I didn't question you the other night when you tried to take me out," answered Ashley.

He grinned and stood up, stretching his long limbs before walking past her towards the bathroom. After last night, Ashley was more determined than ever to get Gabe to do Evan's surgery.

It was risky, and Evan could end up paralyzed, but unlike Drew who thought his life ended because of it, Evan's would be saved. She made them pancakes for breakfast, and they sat in silence across from each other eating. Afterwards, Gabe washed the dishes and she dried them, it was just so simple with him. She loved the domestic side of it all, two people just doing dishes. Ashley grabbed her sunglasses and car keys, fed Ninja, and called Gabe to follow. While he had been in the shower, she had made a phone call and knew that everything would be ready for them.

Ashley parked outside the social services, and Gabe stared at her confused.

"I want to show you something," said Ashley, getting out of the car.

He climbed out of the car and followed her inside. Ashley found Jill and approached her.

"How is she doing?" asked Ashley.

"She is getting so big," replied Jill.

"I want you to meet the man who helped save her," said Ashley.

Gabe looked at her with a stunned expression, taking a step back.

"I did nothing," mumbled Gabe.

"I am glad that you did. Now, would you like to see her? She just woke up," smiled Jill, leading them down the passage. Ashley followed Jill, looking over her shoulder to make sure Gabe was following.

They entered the nursery, and Jill pointed them over to the right crib, before turning to leave. Ashley walked over to the crib, her face lighting up at the sight of Melody. She had grown so much, her small mouth opened in a smile when she saw them. Ashley gently lifted her up into her arms, the smell of baby powder hitting her nose. She turned and, without giving him a chance to back out, slipped the baby into his arms. Gabe looked down at the little girl he had delivered two months ago. Gabe swallowed past the lump in his throat. "Her name is Melody," said Ashley. Gabe's hand shook slightly as he held her in the crook of his arm and let her grab his other finger. He looked up at Ashley with teary eyes.

"Why did you bring me here?" croaked Gabe.

"To show you that you still save lives, you saved her life."

"But she will live in an orphanage. Who says that is better than being dead?" questioned Gabe.

"Look at her! You tell me." Gabe looked down at the wide blue eyes staring back at him, he pinched the bridge of his nose to stop tears from coming out.

"Gabe, you might have walked away from the hospital, but you haven't walked away from being a doctor. For the last three years, you might have thought that Doctor Gabriel Bennett was dead, and maybe for all purposes he is, but Angel Gabriel who saves lives isn't."

Gabe took a deep breath, lifting Melody into his arms.

"Her mother wanted to leave her for the rats," whispered Gabe.

"Instead, you kept her safe and alive."

"Anyone would do that."

"Not someone who would kill someone. You did it to save your friend. It was wrong, but you did it because he asked it of you and you couldn't see him suffer."

Gabe walked over to the crib and placed Melody back inside, her lower lip quivered and opened in a cry. He picked up the pink pacifier and placed it in her mouth, turning to face Ashley.

"Can we go now?" asked Gabe.

Ashley nodded her head and followed Gabe out. They said goodbye to Jill and got into the car. Ashley looked at Gabe as he sat staring out of the windshield.

"I just want to take you to one more place, then I will drop you where-ever you want to go," said Ashley.

He nodded his head, and Ashley let out the breath she had been holding and started the car. They drove in silence, the car radio playing softly in the background.

Ashley parked outside the small coffee shop and waited for Gabe to say something. Instead, he kept silent and stepped out of the car. Ashley got out and followed him inside. Maria's face lit up when she saw Gabe. She ran and wrapped her arms around his stiff figure.

"Señor Gabe, it is so good to see you. The children are with friends today, or they would have loved to see you," cried Maria.

"Hello, Maria. You remember my friend Ashley?"

"Si, I do. She is very pretty. Would you like to sit down and have a coffee?"

"That would be lovely, and then you should tell Gabe what you told me."

Gabe's head shot up, and he gave her a weird look she was unable to interpret. They followed Maria to a table in the back, taking a seat and ordering coffee. She left them alone for a few minutes, to get their coffee.

"Why did you bring me here?"

"To show you that you change lives, you help others," replied Gabe.

"I just gave her advice," replied Gabe.

"Don't lie to me, we both know you did more than that," answered Ashley, sitting back in her chair.

Maria placed a cup of coffee in front of them, smiling the whole time. Gabe hadn't ever seen her so happy.

"Tell Gabe what has been happening the past two months."

"The children are both in school now. Manny is top of his class, and Angie loves to draw, and me. I go back to school at night, I become a nurse and help others like you do," said Maria.

"A nurse! I am impressed, Maria."

"Si, I am doing it for my children. I want them to be proud of their mama. It is all thanks to you."

"No, please, it was all you, Maria," shrugged Gabe.

"I know I did the hard part, but you gave me the courage. You saved my daughter and then my whole family," cried Maria.

"I am just glad that you are all happy and safe."

"Si, but are you happy, Angel Gabriel?" asked Maria, before walking away.

Gabe waited for her to walk away before picking up his coffee and taking a sip. He stared at Ashley over the rim. She sat there beaming, sipping her own coffee.

"Tell me about this patient then," said Gabe, putting his cup down and relaxing back in the chair with his fingers laced across his stomach.

"His name is Evan, and he is fifteen years old," said Ashley, leaning forward with her elbows on the table.

CHAPTER 13

So what is so special about this boy that Dr. Denver can't do it?" asked Gabe.

"He has a tumour on his spinal cord.," answered Ashley.

"Seriously! You know how dangerous that surgery is? My first surgery back and I could kill or paralyze the patient," cried Gabe.

"No one else can do it. They give him maybe a year to live without the surgery. The insurance only works with this hospital and no doctor is willing to come here to do it," replied Ashley.

"I can't promise you I will do this surgery, but I am willing to speak to Zack."

"Really! So you will come out of hiding?"

"I never said that, I said I will speak to Zack."

"Well, I have the perfect solution. Tonight is the annual Doctors-Without-Borders fund-raiser, and everyone will be there. So you will come as my date," smiled Ashley.

"Are you mad? I am trying to keep a low profile, and you want me to appear back from the dead in a fund-raiser with cameras and everything?" cried Gabe.

"Yes."

"Fine, but I could still disappear afterwards again. Now let's get out of here."

Ashley took out her purse, but Gabe stopped her.

"I might be homeless, but I can pay for our coffee," grumbled Gabe.

Ashley laughed and led the way out of the coffee shop.

"If I had still not agreed, what would you have done next?" asked Gabe.

"Taken you to see the guy you saved, Troy."

"What guy?"

"The one with a pen sticking out of his chest."

"I saved his life!" defended Gabe.

"Exactly my point," smiled Ashley.

"So where should I drop you? It starts at seven tonight, and we can't be late."

"I will show you where," answered Gabe, opening the car door.

Gabe climbed out of Ashley's car, and turned to face his house. He turned back to the car and leaned down into the open window.

"This is your place? You chose to live under a bridge than to live here?" cried Ashley.

"We all have our burdens to carry. I will pick you up before seven," replied Gabe.

He waved goodbye and watched her drive away. Gabe stared at the locked metal gate in front of him. He took off the brown coat he was wearing and searched the inner seam until he came across the secret pocket. Pulling out the small set of keys, Gabe opened the gate and walked down the long driveway towards his house. He opened the front door and stepped inside. The place looked just like he had left it. The flooring was laminated wood, and the walls were a cream colour. The entrance had a coat hook that still held his most expensive jackets and a large staircase that led to the upper floor. Gabe jogged up the stairs, walking into the master bedroom. He stared at the large queen-size bed with the black satin bedding and groaned. No wonder people must have thought he was mad, to have given all this up.

He walked through the walk-in-closet, running his hands along the many shirts and jackets hanging up. After three years of owning two shirts, it was weird to have so many to choose from. Gabe threw his brown jacket onto the soft white plush carpets and walked into the ensuite bathroom. Gabe nearly collapsed to his knees and kissed the large spa bath, turning the taps on fully. After a long bath, Gabe stood in front of the bathroom mirror, his white dress shirt hanging open, a bow-tie loose around his neck. He ran a hand along his smooth chin, dabbing a bit of after shave on and tying his long hair back, before buttoning his shirt. It felt good wearing clean clothing, wearing something that wasn't moments away from ripping. He walked out of the bathroom, his bare feet sinking into the soft carpets. He was emotionally exhausted and not at all prepared for tonight. But he would do this for Ashley. He picked up the keys to his red sports car and jogged back down the stairs, his nerves all over the place.

Gabe drove over to Ashley's place, ringing the buzzer. He waited for her with his back against the side of the car, his hands in his black dress pants pockets, and his ankles crossed. The door opened, and he sucked in a breath, letting it out in a loud whistle. She looked beautiful, her blonde hair hung loose forming wavy curls around her shoulders, and she had on a strapless white and black cocktail dress that showed off all her curves.

"You look beautiful," said Gabe, opening the car door for her.

"Thank you, you clean up quite well yourself," replied Ashley, running her fingers along his smooth jaw.

"I haven't been this nervous since Med-school," mumbled Gabe, walking around the car.

"You will do just fine. Besides, these things tend to get boring, and with you there, it will bring something new to liven up the evening," smiled Ashley.

He rolled his eyes and started the car.

Ashley couldn't stop staring at Gabe; he had really thrown her for a loop when he had shown up in that suit.

He had on a black suit that fit him snugly, his hair neatly tied back. He was even more breath-taking than she could ever imagine. She was just as nervous as he was, but she wanted this night to go well. So she had to be strong for him; this could all go horribly wrong if they weren't careful. He stopped in front of the grand hall, handing his car keys to the valet before walking around to open her door. Ashley smiled and slipped her arm through his. She felt him tremble slightly and felt guilt wash over her for pressuring him this much. Maybe it was too soon, she thought. But this was about more than the two, of them; this was about saving a boy's life and maybe many more after that.

"Shall we do this?" questioned Gabe.

She looked up at him; he kept his emotions clearly hidden. She nodded her head and let him lead her up the front steps and into the grand ballroom. It was like every conversation in the room suddenly came to a halt. You could probably hear a pin drop. Everyone was staring at them.

"Guess who isn't dead!" stated Gabe, breaking the ice.

It was like that one comment snapped everyone to attention; surprised whispers and gossip started all over. Paparazzi ran towards them, snapping as many pictures of them as they could. Gabe ignored them and walked straight through the people with her on his arm. He took two flutes of champagne and handed her one. They stood to one side, people still staring at them. Karla walked towards them in a stunning turquoise dress, her expression one of surprised shock. She pulled Ashley into a hug.

"Is this your secret boyfriend? The dead doctor?" whispered Karla.

"As you can see, he isn't actually dead," laughed Ashley.

"Honey, I can see that, and damn, is he fine or what. You will tell me everything about him, and I mean everything, as in him discharging my patient," stated Karla.

"Soon, I promise. And where is my brother tonight?" asked Ashley. "He couldn't make it tonight, but he is taking me home for the weekend to make up for it."

"He couldn't make it tonight, but he is taking me home for the weekend to make up for it."

"You are going to see my parents?"

"It is weird, right?" giggled Karla. With one last look at Gabe, she walked away.

"Well, this is awkward," said Gabe, swallowing the champagne in one gulp. A

shley spotted Zack talking to the chief of residence and signaled him over; he nodded in reply and five minutes later came to join them.

"So that was why you asked me all those questions about Gabe?" laughed Zack.

"Yes, but he hasn't said he would do it yet." Zack turned to face Gabe, his expression genuine.

"It is good to see you alive; Andy must be so happy."

"She doesn't know yet," answered Gabe.

"Oh man, she is going to kick your butt for coming here first," chuckled Zack.

"Yeah, but I guess I deserve it," shrugged Gabe.

"You do. I want to hit that smug face of yours for disappearing like that and causing us to worry.

"Where have you been, man?"

"I was on a much needed sabbatical after the whole Drew thing," lied Gabe. "I'm just glad you are back. Now let us go talk to the chief about getting your job back. I assume that is why you came? And Ashley probably told you about my patient Evan?" asked Zack, his brow arched.

Gabe nodded his head, looking past Zack towards the chief. Ashley touched his sleeve.

"Go talk to him; I will be waiting here," whispered Ashley.

"I will be right back," replied Gabe, bending down and kissing her on the cheek.

Ashley watched him walk away, tension seeping out of her body. She put the empty champagne flute on a passing tray and turned to face the large masses of people.

"I see you brought your thief with you!" said a voice behind her.

Ashley jumped and turned to face Romeo.

"You nearly gave me a heart attack," cried Ashley, slapping him on the arm.

"Ouch," grinned Romeo, with a sheepish smile.

"Besides, he is more than that, and he used the medicine to help people."

"A real-life Robin Hood," teased Romeo.

"He is a really nice guy, and I bet that if you got to know him, you two could be good friends."

"I am just teasing you, Ash. I saw the way he treated you on the day of the shooting. If I ever saw you with anyone, but myself, it would be him," smiled Romeo.

"Thank you," replied Ashley, kissing him on the cheek. Ashley felt a shadow looming over them.

She turned around to face Gabe. He had a threatening look of jealousy on his face.

"I should get back to my date; nice seeing you again, Gabe," said Romeo, walking away.

"You won't make any friends if you scare them away."

"Let's dance," answered Gabe, grabbing her hand and pulling her onto the dance floor.

The music was soft and slow, and she wrapped her arms around his waist and laid her cheek against his chest.

"Did you get your job back?" asked Ashley.

"I don't want it back," replied Gabe. Ashley lifted her head up, staring into his eyes.

"But what about Evan?"

"I asked the chief if it was possible to do the surgery without applying for a job, and he said yes!"

Ashley's face lit up at the possibility of Evan getting his surgery.

"But that still doesn't mean I will do the surgery, Ashley. I still have to speak to Evan and his family," warned Gabe.

"Thank you, Gabe. But what will you do afterwards?"

"I don't know yet," sighed Gabe.

Ashley gave him a small smile, before resting her cheek back on his chest. She let him lead her around the dance floor, feeling safe and happy.

Gabe stood in his state-of-the-art kitchen, staring out of the window at the overgrown gardens and sipping his coffee. He wore a clean pair of denim jeans and a grey button-down shirt with his sleeves rolled up. He had slept wonderfully last night. The sheets were so soft and comfortable. Suddenly, he heard the front door open and then slam shut with force. Gabe turned away from the window. His sister entered the kitchen, her face looking murderous as she carried a newspaper in her hand. Gabe placed his coffee down onto the counter and approached her cautiously.

"This is how I find out you are alive!" yelled Andy, throwing down the newspaper with his photo on the cover.

"Yeah, about that, it was last minute," shrugged Gabe.

Andy walked straight up to him and slapped him across the face. He looked back at his sister with shock. Gabe brought his hand up and touched his inflamed cheek.

"You bastard, disappearing for three years!" shouted Andy.

"I am sorry," replied Gabe.

"You left me alone. I wanted to believe you were alive, but it was so hard. You let me believe you were dead, you let everyone believe that, but why did I have to suffer also?" sobbed Andy.

Her eyes started to fill with tears.

"Sis, I am so sorry for causing you so much pain. I truly am," Gabe stepped forward, pulling her into his arms.

She wrapped her arms around his waist, letting the tears take over.

"I missed you so much. You just disappeared without saying goodbye. I just lost my brother, I had no one but Luke," answered Andy between sobs.

"I know, but I was always watching out for you… always keeping an eye on you," replied Gabe.

"I saw you the night Gabby was born. You were there, and I just knew you were alive still. And I got the flower you left me; you always loved making them. Papa used to say you would win a woman over with those blasted tin flowers," mumbled Andy, stepping back and wiping her eyes.

"Papa was right, you know. Besides, do you think I would miss seeing you become a mother?" smiled Gabe.

"Why did you leave?" questioned Andy, crossing her arms.

"Please don't ask that of me, not right now. And besides, I want to meet my niece," "Oh, I told them to wait in the car," giggled Andy.

Gabe rolled his eyes and placed his arm around her shoulder, steering her to the front door.

"Go get your family; I will make more coffee."

"But don't just disappear again!" pleaded Andy.

"I won't," said Gabe, his expression softening with guilt.

Gabe sat at the table, watching his niece Gabby run around the kitchen while her parents sat across from him.

"If Andy hadn't slapped you, I surely would have! You have caused her many tears over the past three years, and if I didn't know you as well as I do, then I wouldn't understand. But you must have had your reasons. I just wish you had let us know you were alright," said Luke.

"I know, and if I didn't think you were capable of taking care of Andy, I would never have left."

"Enough serious talk. I promised Gabby that we would go for ice-cream in the park, and she would love for her uncle to join us," interrupted Andy.

"Let me just put on some shoes, and I will be right with you."

They gathered their things and all left together in Luke's car. Gabe felt more relaxed than he had in years. Gabby had instantly taken to him and babbled the whole way. She had started to call him 'Unca Jabe', Andy laughed and made her repeat it. At the park, Gabe lifted Gabby onto his shoulders and followed her parents along the path towards the ice-cream stand. They bought ice-creams and sat down near the lake, eating them. Gabby held hers tightly, cracking the cone and causing ice-cream to spill all over. Her face was covered in chocolate, her dress too. She smiled at Gabe, lifting her messy ice-cream for him to lick. Gabe smiled and took a big bite; she giggled.

"Are you going to do the surgery?" asked Luke.

Gabe looked up at his brother-in-law.

"I don't know," replied Gabe.

"I think that you should do it, but only if it means that you won't disappear again," said Andy.

"No matter what happens, you will always know where I am from now on. I was selfish to keep my whereabouts a secret from you and Luke, and I missed out on so much these last few years," answered Gabe.

After that, they lightened the mood, relaxing in the shade while Gabby ran after the birds walking around.

"Aunty Amabel!" squealed Gabby, taking off in a run towards the woman approaching them.

Gabe sat up from his lying position on the grass and looked straight at Annabel, carrying Gabby on her hip and her two young boys trailing behind. Gabe tensed up, as she slowly approached.

"Hello, guys. I was taking the boys for a walk when I saw you all here," said Annabel, setting Gabby down.

Gabe stood up awkwardly, sticking his shaking hands in his pockets. She looked straight up at him. He felt guilt wash over him. It felt suffocating as he looked into her mournful eyes.

"I heard you were alive," whispered Annabel.

"I am sorry, I have to go," mumbled Gabe, turning to leave.

"Gabe! Wait! Please!" yelled Annabel.

But he ignored her pleas and carried on walking. He felt guilty for just walking away from his sister, but he needed to leave. He might have redeemed himself for what he had done, but it still didn't make it right in his eyes that they had lost the man they loved because of him.

He walked towards the bridge and paced back and forth for a while, trying to clear his head. Gabe thought about the surgery he had to perform in a few days and made his way to the hospital. At the hospital, he found Evan typing on his cell phone.

"Evan," interrupted Gabe.

The teen looked up at Gabe, confused.

"Who are you?"

"I am Doctor Gabe Bennett, and I am looking into your procedure for removing the tumour," replied Gabe.

He walked into the room and sitting down in the chair next to Evan's bed. Evan put down his cell phone, his face lighting up.

"Doctor Denver mentioned you. He said you are the best."

"Well, I wouldn't say that, but I have done a procedure similar to this before."

"My mom says if this goes well, I could be back on the soccer team soon.," smiled Evan.

"Evan, this procedure is dangerous, and there is a chance that you could be paralyzed," said Gabe.

"I know, and I am willing to take that chance," answered Evan.

"And what happens if you are paralyzed?" asked Gabe.

"I will still be alive, won't I? It beats being dead," shrugged Evan.

Gabe swallowed past the lump in his throat, nodding his head and leaving the room. He couldn't help but compare the differences between Drew and Evan. Their conditions were entirely different, yet both surgeries stood the chance of paralysis. Yet one patient saw it as a death sentence, and the other saw it as being given a second chance.

CHAPTER 14

Ashley was nervous. She ran a hand through her straight hair, wondering what could have possessed her to agree to a double date with Chad and Karla. Gabe would be there to pick her up in the next ten minutes. They were eating at the new Steakhouse in the city, but she was so nervous that she doubted she would be able to eat a thing. Her buzzer went off, and she groaned out loud, grabbing her red coat and black purse before leaving the apartment. She stepped outside into the cool evening air, where Gabe stood with a metal flower in his hand. Ashley smiled and took it from him.

"Roses are over-rated," said Gabe with a shrug.

Ashley laughed and placed the flower gently in her handbag before sliding past Gabe, who held the door open for her, and climbed into the car. They drove in silence towards the restaurant. Ashley stared at Gabe's profile while he drove. He seemed so calm, but she noticed the way he kept checking his wristwatch to make sure they weren't late. They arrived at the restaurant, and Ashley followed Gabe inside.He led her to a table in the back where Chad and Karla were already waiting.

"Hi, sorry we are late. There was traffic," said Ashley as she sat down opposite Karla.

Gabe slid her chair in for her and held out his hand towards Chad.

"Sorry about the last time we met. I am Gabe, and you must be Chad," stated Gabe, shaking Chad's hand.

"This is Ashley's good friend and my girlfriend, Karla," introduced Chad.

They all sat down and ordered appetizers. Things went downhill from there. The conversation was stilted, and between Chad and Karla's glares, not much was said.

"So Ashley tells me that you are a horse trainer," said Gabe.

"Yes," answered Chad.

"What have you been up to these last few years, Gabe?" asked Karla.

"I was on a sabbatical."

"Oh, really? And what country were you in?"

"Karla! Stop interrogating him," cried Ashley.

"You can't tell me no one is interested in where he has been the last few years and why he suddenly came back."

"Gabe has his reasons," replied Ashley.

"How did you two meet?" asked Chad with a mischievous grin.

"In the street," said Gabe at the same time Ashley said, "at work."

"Well, which is it? At work or in the street?" questioned Karla.

"Both. I was working, and Gabe happened to be there in the street and lent a helping hand. Anyways, enough about Gabe. How is your mom?"

After that, the conversation stayed on safer topics, but Karla kept glaring at Gabe throughout the meal. Ashley kicked Karla gently under the table, giving her a questioning look. Karla just stared back tight-lipped. Ashley pushed her food around her plate. She finally stood up, excused herself, and went to the bathroom. Ashley finished in the toilet and opened the door, to find Karla standing in the bathroom with her hands on her hips.

"Why are you being so rude to Gabe?" asked Ashley as she washed her hands.

"Because he isn't who he says he is, and I don't want you to get hurt," cried Karla.

Ashley dried her hands and turned to face her friend.

"Who is he then?"

"I don't think it is my place to tell."

"No, you brought this up, and you need to tell me what you know," insisted Ashley.

"He has a kid, well, two children," replied Karla.

"What! Gabe does not have children," laughed Ashley.

"Yes, he does. Remember that patient I told you about that Gabe logged out? Well, it was his daughter."

"No, it wasn't. He was helping a friend out. He lied to you."

"And that makes it all better. He isn't a father, but he is a liar," stated Karla.

"No, you are twisting things. Gabe is a good guy, and I swear if you give him the chance, you will see."

"I trust you, Ash. If you say he is a nice guy, then he is. But please be careful," said Karla.

"Does this mean you will stop glaring at him?"

They burst out laughing and hugged each other, before going back to the table to finish their food. The rest of the evening went more smoothly after that.

Two nights later, Ashley sat on the floor with her back against the three-seater, sofa in Gabe's living room. Their empty Chinese food containers lay scattered across the coffee table. She stretched out her legs, rubbing her full stomach. Gabe sat across from her, an open folder lying in front of him with Evan's medical information.

"There is a seventy percent chance that he will be paralyzed," said Gabe with a frustrated sigh, running his fingers through his long hair.

"But it is better than being dead. Zack agrees, and so do his parents," answered Ashley.

"I haven't done an operation since Drew," stated Gabe, slamming the folder shut.

"I know that, but I believe in you, and I think you can save his life," smiled Ashley, crawling across the carpet towards him.

147

He crossed his arms over his chest, staring at her. She grinned and crawled between his open legs, placing her hands flat on his chest.

"I think that no matter what happens in the operating theatre, Evan has a better chance with you as his surgeon than anyone else."

"You have a lot of faith in me," whispered Gabe, leaning his forehead against hers.

"I do, and you need to have faith in yourself," replied Ashley, lifting her head slightly, their lips touching in a slow, soft kiss.

He smiled and pulled back, twirling a strand of her hair around his finger.

"It is getting late, and I need to get an early start, so as much as I love having you right here," said Gabe.

"Alright, you don't have to say it. I will go home, and I will see you tomorrow after the surgery," smiled Ashley, standing up.

He gave her a mischievous smile, pulling on her hand, so that she tumbled back down onto him.

"Is that all I get? A see you after surgery?" asked Gabe.

"Well, what would you like?"

"Maybe a kiss goodnight would suffice." Ashley laughed and wrapped her arms around his neck, leaning forward until their lips met.

The doorbell rang, interrupting them. Ashley laughed and sat back. Gabe stood up and walked to the front door. Ashley heard the door open and a feminine voice. She stood up, running a hand through her hair while she waited for them to appear.

"Hey, Ashley, look who I found outside my door," called Gabe.

Gabe walked into the room with his sister, Andy. Ashley smiled awkwardly.

"We have met already, Gabe," replied Andy, pulling Ashley into a hug.

"I know, but it's different this time."

"How is your daughter, Gabby?" asked Ashley.

She is asleep. She runs around all day and then just drops," laughed Andy.

"Would you like a cup of coffee?" offered Gabe.

"No, Luke will worry where I have gone if I take long. I just came to wish you good luck for tomorrow."

"Thank you."

"And I wanted to thank Ashley in person for giving me my brother back."

"No, you don't need to do that. I didn't do anything," cried Ashley.

"Nonsense, you brought him home. So that makes us sisters, and we should go for coffee soon."

"What about me?" questioned Gabe.

"You can spend the day with Luke and Gabby," smiled Andy before kissing him on the cheek and heading to the front door.

They waited until she left before Ashley gathered up her things.

"I should be going too."

"See you tomorrow." Ashley kissed him on the lips goodbye and made the short trip home.

Ashley yawned and stepped out of her car, jogging up the stairs and entering her apartment. She nearly screamed out loud at the sight of her mother standing in her kitchen doorway.

"Mom! What are you doing here?" cried Ashley, hugging her mother.

She hadn't seen her mother in three years, and hearing her voice on the phone wasn't the same as seeing her in person.

"I came to see you, dear," replied her mother, Michelle.

Ashley stepped back.

"If I had known you were here, I would have come home earlier."

"Well, you are here now, dear. I put the kettle on when I heard your key in the lock."

"How did you get in?" asked Ashley.

"Joel brought me here. He is back at the hotel where we are staying."

Ashley nodded and helped her mother make them each a cup of tea. They took their cups and sat down.

"Ash, I know why you left town, and even though it broke my heart, I am still proud of what you have become," said Michelle.

"Mom." She stopped at the stern look in her mother's eyes.

"Your father was wrong! You both are so stubborn at times that it drives me insane. I have been working on him these last few years, and we had planned to come visit you later in the year. But now your father is too sick, and I don't want him to die without saying sorry to you or for you to say goodbye," sobbed Michelle.

"I don't know what to say," cried Ashley.

"Don't say anything, just think about it. He is still your father, Ashley, and he made a mistake. He thought he was doing it for the right reasons, but he was wrong. He has paid the price for his sins! He lost his little girl, but don't condemn him and let him die without your forgiveness!"

"What do you mean, Mom?"

"I have said too much already. Your father would have a fit if he knew I had come here. If you come home, he will explain everything to you."

"But my whole life is here," cried Ashley.

"Then just come visit, Ashley, just come say goodbye because whether you like it or not, he is dying."

"I will think about it," replied Ashley.

"Good, that is all I ask. Now it is late, and Joel will be worried."

Her mother stood up, kissing her on the forehead before leaving. Ashley sat staring at the door long after her mother left.

Gabe stood next to Zack in Evan's room, his parents and siblings standing next to his bed.

"Doctor Bennett is our best neurologist," said Zack.

"But where has he been? Why has he only turned up now?" asked Evan's father.

"I was on a sabbatical; I had personal issues that I needed to sort out," answered Gabe.

"And are you sure our son will be in good hands? We trust you, Doctor Denver," replied the mother.

"Yes, I trust Doctor Bennett, and I would be honoured to have him perform my surgery any day," Gabe smiled and nodded, leaving the family alone to say goodbye to their son.

"Zack, do you really trust me that much?" asked Gabe.

"Yeah, I do. I don't know where you have been the last three years, but you must have had a good excuse. Now, let's go scrub in," smiled Zack, patting him on the back.

Gabe nodded and signaled the nurses to wheel Evan toward the Operating Room. He followed behind and stood in his blue scrubs washing his hands. He stared through the glass at Evan lying on the table, his heart rate picking up. It had been three years since he had done surgery. The last person had been his best friend. Zack gave him a questioning look. He shook his head, slipped on the latex gloves, and tied his mask over his mouth.

"How are you doing, Evan?" asked Gabe.

"Can't feel a thing," grinned Evan.

"Good, we need to make sure that we don't damage your spinal cord and paralyze you. So this pretty nurse over here will be asking you to move your hands and feet," said Gabe.

Evan nodded his head. Gabe turned toward the screen. He nodded his head, and the catheter injected the blue liquid into his spinal cord, showing them where the tumour was and the different veins running through it. Gabe picked up the scalpel and made a small incision along his lower back, sweat forming on his brow. He needed to work slowly and carefully to avoid any unnecessary bleeds. Gabe started the slow process of removing the tumour. It was pushing directly on Evan's nerves, and one small slip could leave him paralyzed. He made sure to check that Evan could still move his fingers, before continuing. He hadn't realized how much he had missed this until now. Helping someone, by removing harmful tumours was a miracle in itself, and he was grateful for the skills he had, to perform such a task. He was close to finishing off, when suddenly blood started pouring out of the open wound. Evan's blood pressure dropped, and his body started shaking.

"Zack, there is a bleed. I need your help finding it before he bleeds out," yelled Gabe, searching for the artery.

Nurses kept Evan still, as Gabe searched. The boy's heart rate was slowing down. His heart suddenly stopped, the machine beeping long and hard.

"No! Evan, stay with me!" yelled Gabe.

"We need to start compressions," said Zack.

"I need to stop the bleeding, or he won't survive," answered Gabe.

He finally found the ruptured artery and sealed it up before signalling for Zack to start the defibrillator. After being shocked twice, Evan's heart jump-started, and his vitals started returning to normal. Gabe quickly closed Evan up, allowing Zack to take over the rest. He pulled the bloody gloves off and headed for the door.

"Gabe, where are you going?" called Zack.

"He is alive, isn't he? You can finish up here."

"Don't you want to see him when he wakes up?"

"No, just make sure there is no swelling or bleeds, and he will be fine," said Gabe, walking out of the surgery.

He walked down the long hall and into a deserted corridor, collapsing to the floor as he took in deep breaths. The boy had nearly died on his table. Gabe waited for his heart rate to calm down as he kept seeing Drew's lifeless body lying in the bed, Drew's blood on his hands. He stood up and walked through reception, ignoring everyone's congratulations.

"Gabe, I heard it went well," called Ashley.

Ashley watched Gabe walk away from her, barely hearing a word she said. He walked out of the hospital into the pouring rain, still dressed in his bloody scrubs. Something was wrong, she just knew it. She begged Romeo to cover for her; they were doing inventory today, and her shift ended in twenty minutes. Ashley got into her car and drove straight towards his house, the place still dark with no signs of life. She sat in her car, trying to decide where to go next. She turned the car around and drove towards the bridge. Ashley parked her car and took out her umbrella, opening it and walking towards the bridge. She found Gabe standing there. He must have seen her car coming. He stood with his arms crossed, his expression guarded. Ashley stopped just before she got under the bridge, rain pouring onto her umbrella. He ignored her and carried on walking. It was pouring with rain outside. He didn't care; he just wanted out of the hospital, away from all of that.

"Why did you leave, Gabe?" asked Ashley.

"He nearly died," replied Gabe.

"I heard that you saved him. Zack called and told me that he has woken up and has full function of his limbs."

"Well, lucky him," answered Gabe sarcastically.

"What is going on, Gabe? I don't understand!"

"Pretending I didn't kill Drew doesn't go away by not paralyzing someone else."

"And you could lose your license if you come clean about what you did. Let's go home and talk about this."

"I am home, Ashley. Don't you see that? I belong here with these people."

"And why is that?"

"Because I don't deserve a good life!" yelled Gabe.

"Just because you did something wrong, doesn't mean you deserve to suffer forever."

"I am not suffering! I was perfectly content until you came along and screwed it all up!" growled Gabe.

"I screwed it up? I tried to give you your life back!" screamed Ashley.

"Who said I wanted it back!" yelled Gabe, throwing his hands in the air with frustration.

"You did, when you helped those people."

"Look at us, Ashley! We are so different. You out there with your fancy umbrella and me under here with a cardboard box for a bed."

"What makes it so great under there, that you would rather be there than out here with me?" asked Ashley, tears forming in her eyes.

"They accept me for who I am. They don't need more from me but being Gabe."

"I didn't want more either. I just want you," whispered Ashley, tears running down her cheeks.

"Go home, Ashley. Go home to your family. You still have a chance to make a good life for yourself."

"But I love you, Gabe!" sobbed Ashley.

"No, you love the person you're trying to change me into. I am not that man. This is me right here!" yelled Gabe.

"This is my home, along with Lady Bess and Magpie."

"No, this is the prison you have chosen for yourself, and I won't be a part of it. Until you decide you are worth saving, there is nothing I can do."

"Then we agree. Go home and leave me alone."

"I am sorry you can't see what I see. I wish you could see how wonderful you are," cried Ashley, turning and running back to her car. She got into her dry car, turned up the heat, and sat there sobbing. She loved him, and he didn't care. He was happy living under his bridge. Ashley slammed her hands down repeatedly onto the steering wheel, screaming in frustration. Her heart felt like it had shattered into a million pieces, and just the thought of going home alone to her apartment made her cry more. She pulled out her cell phone and called Romeo.

"Hey, did you find him?" asked Romeo.

"Yes, I did," croaked Ashley.

"What is wrong?"

"I told him I loved him, and he told me to go home," sobbed Ashley.

"Oh, Ash, tell me where he is, and I will knock some sense into him."

"No, I think I need to go home for a while, Romeo. I need to make things right with my dad."

"Do you want me to go with you?"

"Thank you, but I need to do this alone," replied Ashley.

After promising Romeo that she would call when she arrived, she ended the call and started her car. She looked back at the bridge once more, staring at the blurry figure she had just lost, before driving away.

Gabe watched her drive away, his own heart breaking. He wanted to run after her and beg her to stay. But he was a mess and he couldn't drag her into it. He turned towards the barrel of fire, sticking his hands out to warm them. Lady Bess stood on the other side, warming her own hands.

"And you are an idiot," said Lady Bess.

"And why would you say that?"

"Because you chased her away, you chose this place over her."

"So what if I did, she deserves more than I can give."

"And who gave you the right to decide for her? I chose all this over my family, and I pay that price every day," cried Lady Bess.

"You could still go home; they want you home, Bess."

"To what? I am sixty years old, I am a recovering drug addict, and if it wasn't for you, I would probably be dead by now. They don't need me; look at them. They did that, their dad did that. I had nothing to do with how they turned out. But you are young and smart, and you have a life to go back to."

"Maybe I don't want all of those things."

"Everyone wants those things, but some of us just don't have a choice. Don't waste your life and don't end up like me."

"I am not listening to this; I need to go get my clothing back," said Gabe, turning to walk away.

"Good, and I don't ever want to see you here again unless it is to visit," yelled Lady Bess.

Gabe ignored her, walking back to the hospital and to his locker for his car keys. He slammed the door shut, finding himself face to face with Romeo. He stepped forward, slamming his fist into Gabe's face. Gabe stammered backward, his face erupting in pain. But he knew he deserved it; he wiped the blood from his lip and stared straight at Romeo.

"You broke her heart," said Romeo.

"I know," answered Gabe.

"So fix it." Gabe turned away from Romeo.

"I wish I could, but she is better off without me."

"Don't ever say that; you made her happy." "I'm sorry," mumbled Gabe, walking away.

He drove home, stopping along the way at a liquor store and buying a bottle of whiskey. He parked the car and walked into the dark house, opening the bottle and taking a large sip. Gabe sat on the bottom step, drinking the whiskey straight from the bottle.

He left the front door open, watching the rain come down. Suddenly a shadow appeared in the doorway, before someone stepped inside and turned the light on. Gabe blinked, as his eyes adjusted to the light, staring at Annabel.

CHAPTER 15

Gabe sat in shock, staring at Annabel, his mind going through all the possible reasons as to why she would be in his house.

"Sorry, the door was open," said Annabel, shutting it behind her.

"What are you doing here?" questioned Gabe, putting down the half-empty bottle.

"I need to speak to you, Gabe." "

About what? The fact that I killed your husband!"

He knew he was being brutal, but he was past caring. He watched her tense up, tears forming in her eyes.

"I cared so much about you, Gabe. You were like a brother to me, and in my devastation over losing Drew, I took it out on you, and I lost two people that day," cried Annabel.

"You were right that day, I did kill him."

"I know." Gabe looked up at her.

How had she known what he had done? Something in his expression must have given his thoughts away.

"Drew left me a note. I received it with the Will. He wrote you a letter also," said Annabel, holding out a worn envelope.

Gabe made no move to take it. She sighed and placed it on the small table with his other mail.

"He was wrong to ask that of you, Gabe. I would have loved him no matter what."

"He didn't want you or the kids to see him like that."

"I was his wife, he should have told me!" screamed Annabel.

"I told him that, I begged him not to ask that of me, but he refused to listen."

"He was stubborn at times, and I am sorry that your life was taken away with his. If Drew learned what had become of you, I think he would be devastated."

"If you are here to ask me to plead for your forgiveness, I won't. I don't deserve it."

"No, I am not here for that. I don't blame you for what you did. I was mad for a very long time at both of you."

"I killed him! He was my brother, and I killed him!" cried Gabe.

"I know, but that is in the past, Gabe. Haven't we all suffered enough? Don't we deserve to be happy?" asked Annabel.

"Why would I deserve that?"

"Because you loved him enough to not let him suffer, and to give up everything that meant something to you."

With that, Annabel opened the front door and left. Gabe stood up angrily and picked up the bottle of whiskey. He threw it against the door, watching it shatter to pieces before grabbing the letter and walking up the stairs.

He walked into his bedroom, dropped the letter onto the bed, and entered the bathroom. Gabe stared at his haggard reflection in the mirror; his eyes were red-rimmed and bloodshot. His hair lay long and limp against his cheeks. He touched his swollen lip, wincing in pain. How could he ever forgive himself after what he had done? He hated what he saw when he looked in the mirror. He slammed his fist into the mirror with enough force to crack it. He did it again and again, until his blood dripped down the basin and the mirror broke in front of him. He stood there heaving angrily, as he stared at himself through the shattered mirror.

He stared at himself through the small pieces of shattered glass, his features contorted. He felt like that inside, he felt like a monster. He washed his bloody knuckles under cold water and bandaged them up before walking towards the bed. Gabe picked up the envelope, his name printed in Drew's neat handwriting on the front. He tore open the envelope and pulled out the letter. Gabe opened the page-long letter, taking a deep breath before reading it.

Gabe,

I am truly sorry for the position I have put you in. You have always been my best friend and brother, and I knew that if I made you promise me, you would do it. Loyal till the end, I don't ever want you to hate yourself or blame yourself for obeying my wishes. In my eyes, you are my hero, my brother, and friend, and I hope you will help Annabel raise my two boys into honourable men like you. I want my sons to be like you, someone who puts others first. You have done so much for others; you were there for me when my parents died and there for Andy when yours died. But no one was there for you, were they? I hope you find it in your heart to forgive me for asking this of you, and please don't blame yourself. I pray that someday you find someone who is willing to put you first and to not let you get away with being so self-less all the time. Gabe, don't ever let this decision ruin your life; you freed me from my pain and let my sons' last memories of me be healthy and happy. I love you, Gabe, and my wish for you is to have the best life you possibly can, and to be the doctor you were always destined to be and to save as many lives as you can.

Your brother, Drew'

Gabe dropped the letter to the ground, falling to his knees as he cried. He had never taken the time to mourn the loss of his best friend. He had been too caught up in his own guilt. He sat on the floor crying, until he had nothing left in him. He finally stood up and walked back into the bathroom, walking towards the shattered mirror and picking up scissors. Gabe lifted up a few strands of hair and cut it off. He repeated the process until his hair was shorter and neater than before.

Then he got into the shower and washed away all the hurt and pain from the last three years. For the first time in a long time, he felt free.

Ashley parked the car outside their ranch in Stone Ridge County. She was exhausted from driving all night long. She just wanted to climb back in bed and sleep for a week. But she needed to do this. She didn't want to end up like Gabe. She didn't want to carry this burden around anymore. She wanted her father back, even if it was for a short amount of time. She got out of the car, yawning and stretching her limbs. Ninja lay curled asleep in the passenger seat. She bent down and lifted the kitten into her arms just as the front door opened, and her mother stepped out onto the front porch crying openly. Ashley smiled weakly and took a step forward.

"I am home," said Ashley.

Michelle burst into tears, pulling her daughter into her arms.

"Mom, you are making it hard to breathe," cried Ashley.

"Sorry, I am just so happy, and your father. Oh, your father!" shouted Michelle.

Ashley laughed through her tears, following her mother inside. She had missed this house; she had grown up here. Chad walked through the side door, his face lighting up when he saw her.

"Ash! You came home!" yelled Chad, lifting her off her feet with the force of his hug.

"Put me down," laughed Ashley.

He chuckled and put her down, taking the kitten from her and leaving her alone with her mother. Her mother answered her unasked question.

"He is lying in bed," said Michelle.

Ashley nodded her head and walked towards her parent's' room,; as a child, she had slept there between them in the large bed. Her dad had kept the nightmares at bay. Her nerves kicked in as she touched the door handle. She wasn't sure what to expect; the last time she had seen him, he had pointed her towards the door. She took a deep breath and turned the handle; the door opened, and she stepped inside.

Ashley stopped and stared, holding back a shocked gasp at the sight of her once strong father lying in the bed, looking fragile and pale. He opened his eyes, a gasp escaping his mouth when he saw her.

"Hello, Dad," said Ashley.

His eyes welled up with tears; she bit back her own. She had never seen her father cry before; he struggled to sit up. Ashley stepped forward and helped her fragile father sit up. He grabbed onto her hand, his shaking slightly.

"Forgive me!" pleaded her father, Charles.

Ashley swallowed past the lump in her throat.

"No Hello, Ashley. How have you been? Just forgive me."

"Why waste time on small talk when we have more important matters to address," croaked Charles.

"Why didn't you believe me?" asked Ashley, tears running down her cheeks. He looked away from her, wiping his own eyes.

"I did believe you." Ashley gasped out loud, yanking her hand free from his.

She stepped back, wrapping her arms around her waist.

"Then why did you say I shamed you?" sobbed Ashley.

"I had to protect you."

"Protect me!"

"From Reed, I needed you to leave."

"But why? We could have gone to the police or something," cried Ashley.

"No, a man like Reed has money, and he would have found a way out of this. I didn't want you near him."

"But you hurt me, I have hated you for three years," screamed Ashley.

"And you were safe," stated Charles.

"Oh, dad, why didn't you just tell me this?"

"Because I am a proud man, and I was stupid and ashamed. I couldn't face you," cried Charles.

"What do we do now?" asked Ashley.

"I would like to hug my daughter if she wouldn't mind." Ashley giggled past her tears and walked towards her father; she climbed onto the bed and slipped her arms around him.

All the tension in her body seeping with the feel of her father's arms wrapped around her. She was finally home.

"I love you, dad."

"I love you, my Buttercup."

"I thought I would never hear that name again," said Ashley.

They stayed silent for a few minutes; her father finally heaved a loud sigh.

"Chad tells me you have met someone," replied Charles.

At the mention of Gabe, Ashley felt tears well up. She let her father soothe her as she told him all about the man under the bridge she had fallen in love with. After that, she fell into an exhausted sleep in his arms, just like when she was a child. She awoke to a dark room, her father still asleep.

Ashley quietly climbed off the bed and slipped out of the room; she heard voices coming from the kitchen and followed the sounds. She walked in to find her two brothers sitting at the table talking in hushed tones. They both stopped talking at the sight of her.

"I see sleeping beauty is awake," teased Chad.

"I drove through the night, Chad," defended Ashley.

"I was just teasing; mom made fried chicken and baked potato," said Chad standing up; he took out a plate from the oven and placed it next to Joel on the counter.

Ashley sat down and groaned out loud at the smells coming from her plate. She heard her brothers chuckle, ignoring them and digging into the food. They both sat there giving each other pointed looks. Ashley rolled her eyes and looked up at them.

"What?" Joel sighed and put his arm around her.

"We want to make a case against Reed."

"What!" screamed Ashley, her appetite instantly disappearing. "He can't get away with this, Ash," cried Joel.

"It was three years ago; no one will believe me."

"Ash, I have found more women, and some of them weren't as lucky as you. They live in fear, and none of them have the guts to leave town like you did. They need someone strong to be their voice," said Chad.

"ME? You want me to speak for all these women?" asked Ashley.

"Yes! We want justice for you and all the other women he has terrorized. He stole you from us for three years," shouted Chad.

"That was my choice to leave."

"We know, but staying wasn't an option with him around."

"How did you find these other women?" questioned Ashley.

"Katrina ended up in the hospital, Ash," replied Joel, anger simmering below the cool surface he portrayed.

"What! Katrina is only seventeen!" cried Ashley.

"She worked for him in the summer. He did such a number on her that I had to pry it out of her. She won't leave the house, and last week she had tried to kill herself."

"Alright enough, I understand. He is a monster, and he needs to be taken down."

"So you will do it?"

"Yes, I will."

Both her brothers smiled and hugged her. She wished she felt as confident as they did. But she had to do this, if not for her then for the others that Reed had hurt.

Gabe woke up in the late afternoon, his head pounding slightly. He got dressed and made himself a cup of strong coffee. Gabe remembered everything from the previous night, including chasing Ashley away. He grabbed a broom and swept up the glass before grabbing a jacket and leaving the house. He needed time to think, away from everything. Gabe strolled through the neighbourhood, walking towards the junk yard. He slipped inside and climbed the pile of junk, sitting on his favourite chair. He looked over at the chair next to him, remembering that the last time he had been there was with Ashley. He sighed in frustration, kicking a loose can with his foot. He sat there for what seemed like hours, before he heard someone behind him. Expecting to see Ashley, he swallowed and turned around, but was surprised to find his sister standing there.

"You aren't leaving again, are you?" asked Andy, making her way up the pile of junk and sitting down next to him.

Gabe carried on making the tin flowers, barely lifting his head up as he worked.

"No, I won't disappear again. Besides, how did you find me?"

"I checked your house and then under the bridge, then I thought of the one place that meant something to you."

"Figures you would be the one person who knew I came here to think," chuckled Gabe.

"I see you cut your hair. It looks good," smiled Andy, running a hand through it.

She collapsed into the chair next to him, digging the toe of her shoe against a rusted tin can.

"So where is Ashley?"

"I chased her away."

"Oh, Gabe! That was a stupid thing to do!" cried Andy.

"I know."

"So what are you going to do about it?"

"I need to become the man she needs me to be," said Gabe.

"But you are already that man."

"You are my sister, you have to say that," shrugged Gabe.

"No, I don't, but I am saying it because I know it is true."

They sat there in silence, staring out at the piles of junk around them.

"Why do you come here to think?" asked Andy.

Gabe looked at her with a wry smile.

"Don't you remember?"

"Of course, I remember, but I want to know why?" replied Andy.

"It makes me remember why I became a doctor in the first place, why it is important to save lives."

"Because you saved mine right here!"

"I didn't save your life, Andy, the doctors did."

"They said if you hadn't done what you had, I would have bled out. As far as I am concerned, you saved me, and you have been saving everyone since."

"I don't know how to save myself," said Gabe, staring down at his shoes.

"Then start at the beginning, start by saving lives again."

"When did you become so smart?" teased Gabe.

"Since my brother decided to pretend he was dead."

"I am really sorry I let you believe that, Andy. You were the one promise I broke."

"No, you didn't break it," stated Andy.

"I didn't?"

"Nope, you stood outside my apartment almost every night," smiled Andy.

"Someone had to keep an eye on you," said Gabe fondly.

"I know, but now you need to sort Gabe out," said Andy, kissing him on the cheek.

CHAPTER 16

3 months later

Gabe walked into the building that had become familiar to him over the last three months. He greeted most of the staff before heading towards Jill's office. She smiled and pulled him into a hug.

"Gabe, it is so good to see you. Melody loves your visits," cried Jill.

"I love spending time with her, but I came to say good bye for a while. I have to leave town for a while, and I know she is still young, but I didn't want to just leave."

"She should be awake still," answered Jill, leading Gabe towards the nursery.

Gabe smiled and walked past Jill, straight towards Melody's crib. The little girl had grown so much in the past few months. Gabe tried to visit as often as he could. He smiled down at Melody and gently lifted her up into his arms. She smiled in return, kicking her feet. Gabe sat down in the chair with her seated on his knees facing him, his hands behind her back for support.

"Hello, beautiful," said Gabe.

She gurgled, her tiny hands opening and closing.

"I won't be seeing you for a while. I have something very important to do, and if all goes well, I will be back to get you."

He bounced her on his knees, pulling faces to make her laugh. After a while, she yawned sleepily. Gabe got her bottle of milk from Jill and sat back down, feeding her as she lay nestled in his arms. He burped her and laid her down in the crib, her eyes drifting closed.

"See you soon, baby girl," whispered Gabe, smoothing a hand through her thick black hair.

Gabe took out a tin flower mobile he had made and tied it above her crib.

"So you will remember me while I am gone." Gabe kissed her on the forehead and left the room.

Ashley watched as they lowered her father's coffin into the ground through tearful eyes. Everything was blurry, and she couldn't stop crying. Her mascara must look a mess, and she must look a mess. After reuniting with her father, she had decided to stay at home for a while, and get a local job in the meantime. In the last few months, she had gotten to know her father all over again, rebuilding their relationship. She had also been busy building her case against Reed. Karla came to visit regularly with Romeo as things between her brother Chad and Karla had gotten serious recently. No one mentioned Gabe, for which she was grateful. She missed him every day, and the pain never subsided. As soon as the case was over, she would go home to New Port. She turned to thank everyone for attending, when she caught a glimpse of a man wearing a brown jacket in the far distance. Ashley excused herself, trying to find the brown jacket that was so familiar to her. Her heart rate picked up as she searched the crowds, but the person was gone. Stopping to scan the area, she finally gave up with the conclusion that she must have just imagined it. She was exhausted, and the last week had been tiring with work, the case, and preparing her father's funeral. She sighed and went in search of Joel, who had taken their father's death the hardest.

Ashley found Joel sitting in the truck, sunglasses covering his eyes. She pulled open the door and slipped inside.

"He is really gone," said Joel.

"I still can't believe it," replied Ashley.

"Mom is holding it together. Better than I hoped."

"She is strong, Joel, we all are. Dad raised us to be independent and strong."

"I know, I just want to go home and be alone right now," answered Joel.

Ashley smiled weakly, turning to look out of the window. She sat forward when she caught a glimpse of the man wearing the brown jacket slipping between the parked cars.

"Did you see that?" asked Ashley.

"See what?"

"That guy wearing a brown jacket!" cried Ashley.

"No one is wearing brown, it is a funeral, Ash. I think you need to go home and sleep for a bit," answered Joel.

Ashley nodded her head, leaning back and closing her eyes. Tomorrow was the court case, and she needed to be on full alert. They had found a total of five girls willing to come forward and testify out of the nine they had spoken to and asked.

Ashley smoothed out her black pencil skirt, took a deep breath, and slipped on her black high heels. Chad honked the car horn. She glanced at her appearance in the mirror once more before running out the door. She slipped into the back seat, her palms sweating as they made their way to the courthouse. Ashley's stomach rolled at the thought of seeing Reed; her nerves were all over the place, but she needed to do this. Chad parked the car, and Joel followed closely behind. Ashley climbed out of the car and took one last deep breath before entering the courthouse. She slipped into the chair next to her lawyer, Amanda Skylark, with Reed at the next table. He glared at her with dark eyes, filled with anger and hatred. She shivered slightly and turned to the front. The judge, an old man who had been in the town for nearly forty year, entered, and everyone stood up.

The proceedings began, and Reed's lawyer gave his opening statement, trying to get the jury to sympathize with the man being prosecuted. Ashley was slightly worried, after that, and Reed flashed her a smug smile. She listened to her lawyer speak to the jury and waited for the next witness to be called.

"We call Gabriel Bennett to the stand," called the lawyer.

Ashley's head shot up, and she searched the courtroom. She gasped when she saw him; he looked so different. His long hair had been cut and styled, and his face was clean-shaven. Gabe made his way to the front of the courtroom, passing Ashley on the way. He looked at her as he passed, causing her heart to beat out of her chest. He sat in the stand next to the judge. Ashley barely heard a word he said, still in shock at seeing him after so long. Afterwards, he smiled at her and sat down next to her brothers directly behind her. Ashley struggled to concentrate after that, knowing he was right behind her. She was called up next and was asked questions by both sides until she wasn't sure what she believed anymore. She was emotionally exhausted, and seeing Gabe hadn't helped. The jury left after that, and they would have their answer by morning. Ashley stood up and hurried out of the courtroom.

Gabe watched Ashley run outside. She looked like she had lost a bit of weight since he had last seen her. He hadn't wanted to upset her by coming, but he had to see her. He wanted her back for good, and he had a plan to do that. He said goodbye to her brothers and made his way outside. Gabe searched the parking lot, spotting Ashley in the distance. She looked distraught and fragile, and he had to fight the urge to walk up to her and take her into his arms. He stood along the side of the building, partly hidden in the shadows. She moved her blonde hair out of her face, tears running down her cheeks. Gabe turned to leave but saw Reed step out from between the cars and approach Ashley. Gabe made his way out of the shadows and headed straight for her. He heard part of the conversation between the two.

"Drop the lawsuit or something could accidentally happen to your home and family," growled Reed.

"Go to hell, or better yet, go to prison. I hear they love rapists there!" spat Ashley.

"Why you little....." yelled Reed as he tried to grab her.

"Don't you dare touch her!" shouted Gabe.

Her startled eyes flew up to meet Gabe's. He clenched his fists and took a step towards Reed.

"And you think you can stop me?" laughed Reed.

"No, we all can," said a voice behind them.

They all turned around to find Chad and Joel standing behind them with their arms crossed. Reed suddenly went pale, holding his arms up in surrender as he took a step back.

"I was just having a nice chat with Ashley," lied Reed.

"We will see what Judge Parkinson has to say about this," stated Joel.

"No! Please!" begged Reed.

Gabe looked back at Ashley once more. She was in good hands with her brothers. He turned and slipped away before she noticed. He stood in the shadows, watching her search the area for him. He felt guilty for leaving her like this, but he had to do this right.

Gabe left and drove to his hotel in town. He had to get ready for tonight. Tonight had the power to change everything. He parked outside her parents' ranch, climbed out of his car, and walked towards the house. He knocked on the door, Chad opening it and pointing him towards the sitting room. Gabe walked through the house and stood in the doorway watching her. She sat in a chair near the fireplace with her feet curled under her. She looked so fragile and small staring into the fire. Gabe coughed softly. Her head turned, and she looked straight at him, her eyes wide with shock.

"I never got to say hello to you today," said Gabe nervously.

"I didn't know that you were going to take the stand. I am sorry if my brother's asked you to speak in court," replied Ashley, her eyes dark with shadows under them.

"They didn't, I offered."

"You did?" asked Ashley, confusion in her green eyes.

"I did," answered Gabe, taking another step into the room.

"Why are you really here, Gabe?"

He watched her wrap her arms around her waist as she withdrew from him slightly.

"I came to see you, Ashley."

"But why? You made yourself clear that day under the bridge," cried Ashley.

"No, I didn't. I was scared and stupid, and I lost the one thing that means the most to me."

"What was that?"

"I lost you, Ashley."

She jumped up from her seat, putting space between them.

"No, don't say that. It has been three months. You can't come here after breaking my heart and say that," shouted Ashley.

"I can and I will, better yet. I will show you," said Gabe, taking off his brown jacket.

"What are you doing?" questioned Ashley warily.

"I chose the streets over you because I thought I couldn't be the man you needed. But you loved me just the way I was, you loved me even though I wore this dirty coat," stated Gabe, walking towards the fire.

"What are you doing, Gabe?"

"This!" replied Gabe, throwing the jacket into the fire.

"No, stop! Why would you do that?" cried Ashley, grabbing the fire poker.

Gabe stepped in front of the fire, blocking her path.

"I am choosing you, Ashley. I am throwing away that jacket which represents my old life and choosing you."

"No! You can't just say things like that!" yelled Ashley, pointing a finger at him.

"I haven't been living on the streets since you left," answered Gabe.

Ashley stopped pacing and stared at him.

"Where have you been living?" "At home, I was busy sorting my life out before I came to tell you that I love you. So that I would be worthy of you, I want to be the man you deserve."

"What are you telling me here?"

"I am here begging you to give me a second chance, to come home with me, please, Ashley!"

Tears welled up in her eyes. Gabe had to fight back his own.

"Ashley, I am sorry, I didn't know coming here would upset you so much." Gabe turned to walk away.

"Wait!" called Ashley.

Gabe turned around, a flicker of hope blooming.

"Do you really love me?"

"Yes, I do. I love how you refused to give up on me and saw the good in me. I love the way you go see Melody even though she is nothing to you and the way you spoke to the other homeless people like they were human. I love you, Ashley, with all my heart, and you make me want to do better."

She walked towards him, stopping in front of him.

"And the streets?"

"Only to visit the people that are my friends, I swear. Besides, it took me this long to come get you because I was turning my house into a doctor's office to help people who can't afford to pay as much for medical attention," replied Gabe.

"You did that because of me?"

"Yes, because I love you."

"I love you too, Gabe," cried Ashley.

His whole face lit up into a smile, he grabbed her and pulled her forward. He wrapped his arms around her and kissed her passionately. She pulled back after a few seconds, her hands on his cheeks.

"I like the short hair," smiled Ashley.

"I thought it suited me better," replied Gabe, running a hand through the short strands.

"If you ever leave me again, the streets will be like Heaven compared to what I will do to you," said Ashley.

Gabe threw back his head and laughed, his arms still wrapped around her. The next moment the door flew open, and her mother ran into the room, hugging them both as she cried excitedly.

"I want lots of grandbabies and a big wedding," cried Michelle.

"Mom! We just got back together!" cried Ashley.

"This man has love in his eyes, he will marry you soon."

"Mom!" hissed Ashley.

"No, your mother is right. I want to marry you, but I first want to date you properly," answered Gabe.

"So trolley racing wasn't an actual date?" asked Ashley with a teasing smile.

Gabe grinned and leaned down to peck her on the lips.

"I have better ideas in mind," whispered Gabe.

Ashley stood in the courtroom, Gabe's hand in hers. She waited for the jury to enter the courtroom, her heart rate picking up. When they finally entered the room, Gabe squeezed her hand and gave her a small smile. They sat down and waited for the Judge to read the verdict. He looked straight at them and opened the piece of paper.

"The jury finds Mr. Reed Silverstone guilty on five accounts of rape, guilty on one account of attempted rape," said the judge.

"But your honour!" screamed Reed.

"That is enough! This is my courtroom!" yelled the judge, banging down his gavel.

"I sentence you to 25 years in prison."

"No!" shouted Reed.

Ashley stood up in a daze, everyone stood up cheering and clapping. Gabe looked down at her with a big smile.

"You did it," said Gabe.

Ashley smiled and let her brothers pull her into one of their bone-crushing hugs. Ashley was finally content; she had Gabe, and together they were starting over.

They went out for lunch as a family, then Ashley showed Gabe around her childhood home till suppertime. After supper, she took Gabe for a trail walk on the horses; he looked like a natural up on the horse. She led them up a hill and stopped her horse, Gabe stopping next to her.

"I used to come here a lot," said Ashley.

"Why?"

"Just wait for it," answered Ashley, smiling. Gabe stared forward.

The sky slowly changed into an array of bright oranges and pinks as the sun slowly set behind a beautiful mountain in the distance.

"Whoa!" said Gabe.

"Nothing beats this," replied Ashley, taking his hand.

"No, nothing beats this. Us seeing the sunset together here," smiled Gabe.

Together they made their way back to the farm, dusk settling around them. They got the horses settled for the night and walked back into the house. Suddenly everyone jumped out from behind the hiding places shouting surprise. Ashley looked around the room startled to find Romeo and Karla standing there with Andy and her family. Even Annabel and her boys were there.

"We thought we would do congratulations on winning the case and getting back together party!" yelled Chad, his arm around Karla.

"Unca Jabe!" squealed Gabby running towards them.

Gabe laughed and lifted the girl up into his arms.

"Gabby, I want you to meet Ashley," said Gabe.

"Hello, Ashley," replied Gabby.

"Hello," smiled Ashley.

They stood together while their family cut cake and spent the evening talking and enjoying themselves. The children were put in spare rooms when they fell asleep, Gabby falling asleep in Gabe's arms. Ashley left him to put the girl to bed and stepped outside. She stood with her arms leaning on the porch railing. She heard someone step outside and turned to smile at Gabe. He walked up to her and stood behind her with his arms around her waist.

"I love you, Ashley," whispered Gabe, kissing her neck.

"When I first saw you walking down the road with your trolley, I never thought we would end up here," replied Ashley.

"I thought you would call the police because I was stealing."

"Never," giggled Ashley's.

She turned in the circle of his arms so that she could face him.

"What happened to your trolley?" questioned Ashley.

"Well, you see, there was this girl, and well, she was being kind of silly."

"Really? Go on."

"And she followed me down an alley where two men were waiting for her, so I, being the hero, had to give up my trolley and save her life."

"By saving her life, do you mean taking her to a strip club?"

"I was worried she was taking life too seriously, and I needed to show her that there was more to life."

"Go on, I have to hear this one," replied Ashley.

"I have nothing, but the look on your face that night was priceless," laughed Gabe.

Ashley joined in laughing, moving her hands up and around his neck.

"Let's stick to saving lives."

"Nothing would make me happier," answered Gabe.

EPILOGUE

Five years later

Ashley stood in the bedroom surveying the mess. She rubbed her hand over her swollen belly, wondering where to start. Her daughter walked into the bedroom, pulling a face.

"It's messy," cried Melody. Ashley smiled and ran a hand through her daughter's black curls. They had adopted Melody shortly after getting married, and she brought sunshine to their life with her bubbly personality. Every day she thrived and learned something new.
"I know. Your brother Drew really knows how to make a mess," laughed Ashley.

"My room is clean," replied Melody.

Her three-year-old son walked into the room, looking like a miniature version of his father, and pulled a face at the mess in front of him.

"Don't pull that face, young man. It is your mess," cried Ashley.

Her three-year-old son walked into the room, looking like a miniature version of his father, and pulled a face at the mess in front of him.

"Don't pull that face, young man. It is your mess," cried Ashley.

"I wanted my superhero top," defended Drew.

"And did you find it?"

"No!" cried Drew, his lower lip wobbling.

"I will help you," declared Melody.

"Alright, you two sort through this, and I will go start with that side of the room," answered Ashley.

She was more exhausted these days, with Drew's endless energy and the baby a month away from being born. She bent down and picked up a discarded shir. Drew was going through a superhero phase and only wore his printed shirts, but he made such a mess that he lost them half the time. She sighed and sat on the bed, folding clean clothing, praying that this child would be calmer like Melody. She loved her daughter so much. She watched her two children work together as they cleaned up the room. Drew jumped up excitedly, waving a red t-shirt around.

"I found it!" shouted Drew.

"Yay," clapped Melody.

"Now we can go see daddy!" replied Drew, hugging the shirt to his chest.

"Not until this room is clean," replied Ashley. She watched the two of them pout and had to hide a grin, keeping a stern expression on her face.

Gabe sat at his desk, filling out the last prescription for the day. He had been busy all day with patients, and after a year of being open, Zack had joined them and made the load easier. With two kids and a pregnant wife, he had endless drama and fun at home, but he loved it all. He didn't regret one minute of his decision. Maria was one of the nurses who worked for them, Manny helped with reception on weekends, while Angie played with the kids. Karla was on maternity leave at the moment, taking care of her twin girls. Chad was the proud, nervous father, who adored his family.

Gabe sat back in the chair, looking at the clock. He watched as Ninja slowly walked into the room and sighed. Only one person would let the cat in, he thought.

"Melody!" called Gabe.

Her black head of curls popped around the corner, her smile bright.

"Yes, daddy?" asked Melody.

"Why is Ninja in here?"

"Because he missed you," answered Melody.

Gabe smiled and opened his arms. She ran towards him, and he lifted her up onto his lap and kissed her on top of the head.

"What are you doing later today?" asked Gabe.

"Mommy is taking us for ice-cream with Gabby, Joe, and Aunty Andy," shouted Melody excitedly.

"That sounds nice. What flavour are you getting this time?"

Melody had the habit of trying a new flavour every time she went. She had a chart in her room and ticked off each new flavour she had tried. She scrunched up her nose, pushing her glasses back up.

"I haven't tried blackcurrant yet."

"That sounds like a nice flavour."

"I want the chocolate one!" shouted Drew, running into the room.

"He always takes chocolate," stated Melody.

"Chocolate is nice," replied Drew, sticking his tongue out.

"Drew, be nice," scolded Gabe.

"Sorry, daddy,. Davie and Cullum always take chocolate, and they are super old," said Drew.

"Super old?" laughed Gabe.

"No, Gabby said eleven and ten are not old," stated Melody.

"Is too. Daddy, tell her I am right," sulked Drew.

"How about we go find mommy," answered Gabe, lifting Melody up and onto his hip as he walked out of the room.

He walked through the rooms looking for his wife. He found her standing in the kitchen with her back towards him.

"Hey, Ashley, what's wrong?" asked Gabe, placing Melody on her feet.

She turned around with a pained expression on her face.

"My water just broke. The baby is coming," said Ashley.

Gabe stood there for a few seconds, trying to process what she was saying. He had heard her, but it wasn't sinking in.

"Gabe?"

"The baby is coming! We need to go get a doctor. Yes, that is what we need," mumbled Gabe.

Ashley smiled and soothingly touched his arm.

"You are a doctor."

"I know that, but the baby is coming, and we need... I can't think. Are you alright? Are you in pain?"

"Gabe, calm down, honey. Andy is on her way with Gabby and little Joe. They will go to the park with the kids while we go to the hospital."

"Yes, that is a good idea."

"Good. Now, why don't you get my hospital bag and explain to the kids what is going on?" Gabe nodded his head and ran out of the room.

He stopped and ran back into the room, giving Ashley a kiss on the lips.

"The baby is coming," whispered Gabe, placing his hand on her stomach.

The front door opened and closed, Andy's voice filtering through the house.

"Ashley, are you ready to go?" called Andy, entering the kitchen.

She was busy digging through her handbag as she headed towards them.

"I left Joe and Gabby in the car, and you know how those two get when left alone for long. Who would have thought that a seven-year-old and a four-year-old could get up to so much mischief......" said Andy, stopping mid-sentence after looking up at them.

"I am having the baby," smiled Ashley, her hand on her stomach.

"Oh! The baby! That is great. Don't worry about the kids; they can sleep at my place tonight."

"Tell the kids we love them, and we will call as soon as the baby is born, I promise," answered Gabe, kissing his sister on the cheek and pulling Ashley by the hand out of the room gently.

Ashley stopped him in the entryway, placing a hand on his cheek tenderly.

"Now, let's go have a baby, and Gabe."

She waited for him to look at her.

"We do what we always do."

"Save some lives," replied Gabe, placing his hand over hers on his cheek.

.

www.ingramcontent.com/pod-product-compliance
Lightning Source LLC
Chambersburg PA
CBHW070031120726
47909CB00003B/1127